Tina's Escapades

Safira English-Sims

THE AUTHOR

www.SafiraEnglishSims.com

ISBN: 978-1-7366695-0-1 (Paperback)
ISBN: 978-1-7366695-1-8 (Hardcover)

Printed in the United States of America
First printing edition 2021

This book is dedicated to Stella Sullivan, Aretha English, Derricko Sims, Amari Varner, Darion Varner, Zyria Varner, Quanesha Dimming-Curry, Brandon Curry Jr., my angels that have gone to heaven, and a host of supportive family & friends whom I appreciate and love beyond life.

Tina Fowler

Chapter 1

In the eyes of the world, I may appear to have it all together. I have the big house over the mountain with the white picket fence, the Range Rover, Bentley and Ashton Martin parked in the driveway. My husband Davion adores me and worships the ground I walk on. We have three of the most intelligent and talented kids anyone could wish for. Money isn't a thing to us because my husband has a multi-million dollar property management company and I'm the owner of the only African American million-dollar hardware store chain in the United States.

You would think that enjoying the finer things in life, being able to travel around the world and having a lovely family to come home to would be enough for me right? That happens only in a perfect world and that world does not exist. Although my husband is one of the sweetest men I have ever met, he is boring as fuck. Trying to have a conversation with him and getting him to understand me is like pulling teeth. We are always so busy with work and kids, having sex is of course a thing of the past. I would try to take him on a date just to put the spark back in the relationship and he would end up spending most of his time looking at his phone. I often wondered who it was that was taking care of his needs because most of the time he was mentally closed off from me. He would always come home and not hang in the streets and he would always hold me tight as we slept. Sex was a no go, we would just come and go and definitely not with each other.

Now do not get me wrong, I'm more than grateful for the life I've been blessed with but what's a girl to do when your "perfect" life isn't so perfect?

Chapter 2

I t was a Monday morning and I headed out the door to work. I never walked around acting entitled, I still had the mindset of going into the stores and being hands on as if I was an hourly associate. I kissed my husband goodbye and told him to enjoy his day at work. I went into our kid's room and made sure I woke them up so they could get ready for school. They were older so they knew how to get themselves ready and out the door on time. All of my kids are mama's babies so I had to take a little time to hug and kiss each one of them before I dashed out the door. I was replaying in my mind what all I needed to accomplish that day to set the tone for the week. Monday's were always my busiest day, in the life of retail I knew that I would be walking into call outs, customer complaints, and long weekly agendas. A part of me wanted to stay at home in bed because my husband made enough money to sustain our lifestyle but the workaholic in me was loyal to the company because it was my baby. I worked my way up in another company and capped off because the upper management team was not diverse, I was an unprivileged black woman. and I was not sleeping around with the people at the top. It motivated me to start my own shit and ensure diversity was a part of it. I had a point to prove and I wanted to make sure others didn't experience what I did so I decided to see it through plus, I couldn't wait to get half way through the day so I could see fine ass Jerome come through those doors. Jerome was my associate that worked only on Saturdays and Sundays because he was the program director of the local boy's and girl's clubs in the area Monday through Friday.

Like me, Jerome had the picture perfect life with a wife and three kids who he meant the world to. He really did not have to work there but he motivated me and helped me start my business. He was mentally invested in the business as well and I paid him a large chunk of change and pussy for all of his support. He was working on a project and I had told him to meet me at the store mid Monday so that I could donate some items to them. Sure, enough around twelve noon he came be-bopping through the doors with the sexiest smile I had ever seen on a man's face. That man was fine! Jerome stood just 6'1, he had a good height, penis size, and personality. Throughout the years he had always made sexual advances at me, most of the time I would shut him down. Three times out of the 18 years we worked together, I had given him a sample because when he really applied pressure, he was irresistible.

That day had turned out to be what seemed like the busiest day of the year and I completely forgot that Jerome was coming so when he walked in, I was caught off guard. I was standing down the aisle looking at fine young ass Kelton flirt with me. I was always professional and it wasn't like I was running around, sleeping with the store. There was no way that I could have a bad reputation. I have always had a nice figure with some ass in the back but I was a lot older so I couldn't understand why and how Kelton had the courage to come on to me. Especially since I was his manager. He was 24 and I was 38, all those young girls running around and he was laying it heavy on me.

"Pop, whatcha doing up here today" Kelton looked past me and yelled. Before I could turn my head to see who he was talking to I heard Jerome's voice say, "Hey son, just trying to handle some business for the school."

My heart dropped in the pit of my stomach because at that point I had just realized that I had fucked the daddy and the son!

Chapter 3

Kelton came on to me harder than any other guy had before. I became so interested in what was between his legs because he was too confident.

Seeing that he was so young, it's safe to say that my curiosity was piqued and I wanted to see what he had going on. I mean hell, he was talking a good game and I wanted to see if his dick game could back up those words. I mean yeah, I did fuck his daddy in the past but it wasn't like I knew they were related. Neither of them were my man and I'm like 95% sure that my husband was fucking somebody else too. He damn sure was not fucking me. If I waited for my husband to make love to me, I would have spider webs between my legs. Like the old saying goes, what you will not do another man will and 9/10 he will do it better.

I had to play it cool but I could not believe what I was hearing. Jerome knew me like the back of his hand so he knew something wasn't right because of the expression on my face. He was a laid back, chill type of guy so in true fashion he kept it cool. "Jerome, all these years we've known each other, I didn't know you had an older son" the words came fumbling out of my mouth. I quickly looked at Kelton and said, "You surely didn't tell me Jerome was your Dad"

Kelton was a young smart ass so he followed up with a "and you didn't ask me bih". He chuckled and tried to laugh it off, but like him, I am a hot head so before I could gather my thoughts, I told him, fuck him and told Jerome that I would meet him in my office. I left the father and son standing on the aisle going at it about respect. I had heard enough and that day I did not have time for Kelton's disrespectful ass. Being a great fuck was something he got from his Pops but his attitude had to come straight from his mammy!

I stormed in my office and closed the door; I text Jerome and told him to get his ass in my office immediately. As soon as he stepped in, I told him to lock the door. He knew what time it was so he instantly got on hard. As he walked over to me, I stood up and pulled my skirt up. Jerome picked me up by my ass and sat me on his hard, fat, long penis. I rode that shit until he burst all in me. I jumped down, licked him clean, and kissed the tip of his dick. Like his son that shit drove him crazy. He started making loud noises so his ass had to go. "Jerome there's the list of items we will be donating to your organization, stop at the customer service desk and have Mavis set up your delivery" I stated as I was

7

getting myself back together. I was done with him and I was ready for his ass to go because I was still mad at his disrespectful ass son. "Alright Tina, I'll see you this weekend. He walked out with a grin on his face. I got up and locked the door behind him because I did not want to be bothered, I had to gather my thoughts. All I could think was, what have I gotten myself into. If Kelton knew that I had been sleeping with his father, he would kill me. He would not care if it was before him, he had anger issues and he was extremely controlling. I had made up my mind that I wasn't going to tell him but I knew I had to tell Jerome. Before anything we were friends and I had a tremendous amount of respect for him. Jerome was understanding, in all the years I had known him I had never seen him angry. He had never disrespected me. There was no way I could sleep at night without talking to him. I just did not know when or how I was going to come clean.

Chapter 4

While sitting in my office doing some paperwork 3 weeks prior, there was a knock at my door. Come in! I yelled looking up to see it was Kelton standing there. I am not going to lie I was checking him out. That boy was fine standing about 6'3 with muscles in all the right places. That brown skin and long dreads down his back did something to me. He had on a black V Neck short sleeve shirt that showed off his tattoos on his arms with dark blue jeans on. All that was going through my head was damn daddy come here so I can take a bite out of yo sexy ass. I was brought out of my thoughts when I heard a low deep chuckle coming from him. You know you can go on and take a picture I will not mind; you can even use it to pleasure yourself tonight when you are in bed. Kelton's young ass was something else and I think he knew it! Rolling my eyes with a slight smile on my face I told him to come in and tell me what he needed. Without wasting any time, he closed the door behind him and sat in the chair across from me. The look in his eyes told me I already knew what he wanted to talk about. I sat back waiting for him to bring it up. With the door closed we knew for sure that nobody would hear what we were talking about. Kelton started looking me straight in my eyes. It was so intense and I had never had anyone look at me like that, he made me feel like he was looking at my soul. Hell, I felt like he could see my thoughts. I could not help but blush at him. "I know you think that it's a joke when I say the things I say to you but in all honesty it's not. I am a grown ass man and I always go for what I want. I know that you are older than me, but you know that age isn't nothing but a number when it comes down to all the things I want to do to you. You know I am not one to sugar coat shit I been wanting you since I first saw you. I ain't got a girlfriend but if I did, I would not care. I know you got a husband but I don't give a damn about him. Just give me a chance and I swear you won't be disappointed." I sat there looking at him for a few moments processing what Kelton had just said to me. From the first time he saw me he laid it on me heavy, I always brush him off. I loved my job and I had worked my ass to get my company, the last thing I wanted to do was get caught up fucking on some young ass boy and losing everything. My husband would kill my ass and the last thing I wanted to do was add another person to the list of men I had slept with. My husband was the first person I had sexually been with and even though I was cheating; my number was still low! I had no desire to have sex with multiple partners. I was proud of myself when it came to that. I could not resist him though, I looked at him and said, bring yo ass over here and give me that dick. I could see the shock in his eyes that I had finally said yes, his eyes lit up with the smile that came across his face. You gotta realize I am a grown ass woman and just like you I don't sugar coat shit myself so if you bad you gone know and if you're good you gone know that too. I am just giving you a heads up. Kelton walked up to me and pulled me to my feet. He kissed me with the softest lips I had ever felt. All it took was one kiss to let me know that I was fucking with a pro! I slide his pants down after he unfastened his belt buckle. He pulled my pants down and stuck his fingers in me, took them out and licked them. Hell yeah, my type of guy! That shit made the kat trap so wet I knew I was about to rock his world because my pussy was waterfall wet. Kelton turned me around and pushed me on my desk. He stuck his penis in me so fast I know he didn't even get a chance to see what it looks like, nor did he have time to put on a condom. I did not expect him to have a large dick because a lot of times he wore them tight ass pants the young kids wear now days. I don't know where it came from but when he inserted himself in me, I thought, "whoa!!" he got dick baby!

"Got damn yo pussy super wet" Kelton moaned. "I know it is daddy now fuck the shit out of me like" I moaned

11

right back. As soon as the words left my mouth Kelton was having an orgasm. I turned around and dropped to my knees and sucked every drop of cum off his dick. I looked up to him and moaned out, "round two, daddy". This was not about to be it. He snatched me up, threw me back on the desk, and went crazy in me. We went for what seemed like hours and as soon as he looked like he was about to cum, I pulled him close to me and whispered in his ear...cum in my wet pussy baby and that's just what he did. He fucked me so good that second time that when we finished my legs were shaking all over the place. I didn't know how long this shit was going to last but I knew I damn sure didn't want it to end anytime soon. I was hooked!

Chapter 5

Being a mom to 3 kids and a wife while owning multiple stores all over the country was mentally and physically draining. Anyone that is required to travel often knows it is hard to get accustomed to balancing work and home life. Somehow I made sure that the kids went to every sports event, school event, and doctor's appointment. Davion worked so much that he hardly had time to see the kids so I tried to make sure I picked up his slack. On days that he did have time to spend with us he showed a balanced side of being comforting and nurturing. He cleaned the house, cooked for us and would even bring my dinner to me while I laid in bed watching television.

"Baby, do you want your food now or do you want to wait", Davion asked me while I was trying to catch up on the last episode of Basketball Wives. "I'd rather have you right now and that food later husband". I always tried to flirt with my husband every chance I got because I was always hopeful that we would work through our issues and get our relationship back to where it used to be. Davion gave me the driest chuckle I'd ever received and quickly dismissed my ass. "You so crazy girl, imma put yo food in the microwave, just let me know when you're ready for it". He leaned over and gave me a peck on the lips and walked back down stairs to finish with whatever he was doing. Situations like that, were my reasons to justify why I felt the need to have relationships with other men and ultimately give them my body. Davion had mastered playing both sides. He would be so attentive and neglectful at the same time. He was the sweetest man I would ever know but when it came to making his wife feel wanted and desired, he definitely missed the mark on that! He was also very secretive at times. It only took a couple of hours of us being around each other for me to be over his ass. That day was no different so I rolled over and text Kelton's fine ignorant ass.

Hey you, what are you up to? I am bored "AF" and you came across my mind. Do you work tomorrow?

Kelton responded:

What up, I am lifting weights with my boy Von...why are you bored, where yo man at?

I responded:

Don't worry about my man, worry about yourself! *And you better not tell Von that you are talking to me.* You work tomorrow? I need some dick...

Kelton responded:

Chill out girl I gotcha ...yeah I'm scheduled in early. You gone have to start paying for this, I can't keep giving it to you for free lol.

I responded:

Damn I never had to pay for it, I'm getting that dick for free. You don't even fuck me enough for all that, I'll see you tomorrow big head.

Kelton responded:

That's what's up OG, good night.

Our conversations were always short and to the point. We never talked on the phone unless something was going down at work and Kelton had to fill me in on the details. I always initiated our text messages but when we did text he was always a different person than he was in person. Whenever we talked about real life things besides sex he was very mature. He was skilled at listening and having a mutual dialogue. Because he was younger than me, I often found myself schooling him about life and he would be extremely receptive to the things I would say. Those qualities drew me into him.

I put my phone on the charger then went and kissed my babies' good night. I got back into my bed and laid there imagining what I was going to do to Kelton, what he was going to do to me, and what location the steamy sex was going to take place. After so many times his young ass had been disrespectful, I could not believe all he had to do was say open sesame and my legs would part like the Red Sea.

Chapter 6

"Mrs. Davis, we need you at the customer service desk immediately" I heard Karen's voice come over the intercom. Karen was my head cashier at my local store, she was often quiet but the tone of her voice was alarming and I knew something extreme was going on. I was in the back of the store going over plans to better organize the store's receiving, so I had to make a quick dash to the front to find out why I was so urgently required to come up front. As soon as I hit the top of the line. I could hear Wendy, my customer service supervisor, "You got me fucked up, I may be white but I'll show you how a white girl gets down bitch. Fuck you and your books, you stupid bitch."

I didn't know who she was talking to at first but I quickly realized that she was talking to one of the part time cashiers, Cassandra, who hadn't been with the company long.

Cassandra was young, in shape, in the military, and not one to play with.

"You ain't nothing but a crackhead ho and you know you took my books. I don't care what color you are; I'll drag you ho."

I had heard enough, I quickly separated the two, I pulled Cassandra in the office with me to talk to me and write a statement. I had my assistant store manager, Gustavo, take Wendy to the training room and do the same.

By the time we had made it into my office Cassandra was crying mad.

"Cassandra, I need you to calm down and tell me what just happened out there. You two ladies just made a scene in the front of my store with customers present." I stated.

Cassandra began to explain to me that she had been down on the lumber register working on her homework because we were extremely slow and she had nothing else to do. Out of nowhere that stupid bi… I mean girl, came in and started talking mess to me.

She said Wendy stated, what yo lazy ass doing here and who told you that you could sit down here like you're on break. I told her that we were slow right now so I thought I would get some of my work done and if that was a problem, she could have professionally told me so. I was so mad that I told her I needed to go to the restroom. When I came back to my register, my books were gone and so was Wendy. I had the cashier Wendy sent down there, cover me and I went to find Wendy. I knew she had taken my books. When I walked up front, she was standing there talking to another cashier. When she saw me she started laughing. I know she took my books, so when I walked up to her I asked her where were my things. She started getting smart talking about she didn't have my books and that I needed to get back to the register before she sent me home. That's when we started cursing each other out and you walked up.

Cassandra should not have been using the company's time to do her homework but Wendy was dead wrong for the way she approached her and handled the situation. Wendy was a very conniving and manipulative bitch so without a doubt I knew she had taken Cassandra's school books. I had to have a conversation with Cassandra about not doing homework again but let's be real, I'd done way worse so I wasn't stressing it. I was definitely firing Wendy's ass because I didn't like her entitled ass any way! The only reason she had been hired was because she had been sleeping with a manager at another store and they had to move her. Only two people knew I owned the company and everyone else thought I was just a store manager, including her ass. She never liked me and always talks shit about me behind my back. If I was nice to her she would talk shit, if I didn't acknowledge her she would talk shit. If she knew that I was THE HEAD negro in charge, I have a funny feeling she would have become a dick rider! I never forgot how she and her buddies treated me. Although I never was going to target her, any fucking thing she did wrong was going to cause her, her job!

I called her into my office and let her know that her actions were appalling and that she was terminated. She left pissed but I didn't give a damn, checkmate hoe!

I clicked on my phone line and called up Quincy.

Hey papi chulo, what are you up to!

Chapter 7

What's up Quincy? About five minutes later he replied, MOMMA, what up my G, shid I'm setting up this bar for an event tonight. Mane, my stomach boiling like a mutherfuka, a nigga asshole on fire...hahaha. Quincy has always been about his money so I've always understood when he was busy. As busy as he was though, he would always hit me back up and the conversation would always include how he had to do the number 2! He was funny as hell and I loved everything about him. Quincy has always been the love of my life. Nobody could or would ever have my heart like he does, what got in our way was bad timing and life. He has always been a real one and has never been one too afraid to put me in my place with the quickness! I always knew he came from a place of love and he wanted me to be the best version of myself. I didn't want to take up too much of his time so I texted him and told him to hit me back up after he was done and ready to leave the club.

I hit Kelton up and told him to meet me in fifteen minutes at his apartment. He texted back with the quickness, bet.

I pulled up in the parking lot of Kelton's apartment complex. I was looking around because I didn't want anyone to notice or see me getting out and going up to his door. He opened the door and slammed it shut behind me. Kelton threw me up against the door and took all my clothes off, I was instantly wet! He got down on his knees and slide his tongue into my throbbing pussy. After licking and sucking on my clit, he looked up at me and moaned, "this is my pussy and you better not ever forget that". He turned me around and slide is tongue in the crack of my ass, his tongue went to all in the right places. I moaned in pleasure, this little boy was turning me the fuck on and I loved every bit of it. As he stood up I put my hand down on his boxers and he was hard as a rock. Kelton threw me down on the stairs and preceded to try and fuck my tight wet vagina. I guided him right to my asshole and popped it on his dick like I was twerking at magic city. Because I was so turned on by him, the hole was wet . He quickly lost control, "damn baby, I ain't never got no ass this good. You give my shit away and I'm gonna have to kill yo ass." I slide his dick out and put it in my pussy. After doing that three times in a row, Kelton had the best orgasm he had ever had in his life.

I had that young ass boy's nose wide open and mind gone!

He grabbed me by the arm and pulled me up to follow him to his room. I sat my naked ass down once we reached his bed. Kelton stood in front of me as I was looking down at his penis. He grabbed me by my neck and said, "I'm not playing with you Tina, this is my shit remember that or I'm going to have to break your damn neck." Kelton was the type to not give a fuck, I had no doubt that he would try some shit like that but I kept in mind he hadn't ever had pussy as good as mine. These young boys didn't know how to act right and always wanted to stake claim quick. I looked him in her eyes and said, "This my pussy and I just let you use it from time to time, if you want this to be yours you gone have to grow the fuck up and boss up. You talking about this your pussy, boy please, I bet you tell your baby mama the same shit. You're disrespectful as hell with your mouth and you couldn't pay half of my bills for this to be yours! You gone have to boss up lil' daddy before you try to claim a bitch like me."

He looked me dead in the eyes after letting go of my neck. He said, "Bitch, get the fuck out my house." You could tell he had never had a woman who wasn't afraid to stand up to him the way I did. I hurt his ego and pissed him all the way off. One thing he was going to learn about me was I would never be cowered down, controlled or used to boost his ego so if he wanted me to leave that was no problem. I went down stairs and grabbed my clothes. He stood at the top of the stairs waiting for me to beg him to let me stay. He'd be standing there for fucking ever waiting on that. I looked up at his naked ass and said, "thank you for the dick." as I walked out the door, I slammed that bitch as hard as I could behind me. I'd see him tomorrow cause this pussy was too good, I'm was too good to him, and I had his nose wide open for him to leave me alone!

Chapter 8

I walked to my car, looked at my phone and noticed I had a missed call from Quincy. I was going to hit him back but I'd noticed it was 3:15pm. My kids were on their way home from school so I needed to make sure that my husband was going to be there until I made it. As soon as I dialed Davion's number, it went to voicemail. I called him back to back 6 times and on the 7th call, he finally answered. "Why the fuck is you not answering your phone Davion?" I said. He replied, "Damn baby, it's been real busy around here, I didn't have my phone so I couldn't hear it ringing. What's going on, what do you want?" I let him know the reason why I was calling and before I could finish my statement, he cut me off. "Shit Tina, Listen I won't have time to make it over there, I got shit to do here and money to make so they'll be straight until you get there."

It was always my husband's responsibility to be at home when the kids got there because he was closer to them, he could come and go as he pleased and it had become perpetual. Today he was busy, my intuition told me that someone had interrupted his responsibility. I was too busy getting my groove back like Stella, I couldn't put my finger on exactly what or who he was doing. I knew that we both were playing one hell of a game and sooner or later, a joker card was gonna show up to play.

Before I could utter another word, he hung up the phone. I was pissed but I had already had one hell of a day. I was over the stupid as men in my life. I dialed Quincy's number back, put my car in reverse, and headed home to my babies.

"Sorry I missed your call papi, how is your day going?" Every time I got myself into some shit that I wanted to quickly be back out, I always thought of how badly I missed Quincy's ass.

"Hey Momma, so you finally called me back with ya fat booty ass huh, hahaha", he said.

Because I was always able to be open and honest with him about everything I was doing and going through, everything that happened that day bolted from my mouth. I told him how I fired that bitch at work and enjoyed every bit of it. I let him know how I fucked Kelton's brains out then got put out, then I told him about Davion's neglectful ass.

"Bra, first of all, your muthafuking ass is tripping! It ain't never like you to be happy about firing a bitch. I know how them folks treated you and shit but, you have always been the bigger person and let that shit go! She definitely deserved to be fired but you wrong as fuck for being happy about the shit Tina." I was only called by my name when he was dead ass serious about whatever he was talking about so I stayed quiet and continued to listen because I knew that he was speaking straight facts! "I'm gonna let yo ass know right now, you need to leave that young ass nigga alone my nigga cause I'm gonna blow his whole block up behind you! I know you're caught up right now and you like what that lil young nigga is doing right now, but Momma that ain't it and he is stupid as fuck to say yo pussy his...hahaha, nigga fuck you talking about. That niggah trippin! Now for yo husband, oh that muthafuka definitely got a shawty on the side but bra that niggah been dropping the ball with yo ass on everything. Now he like fuck the kids and that's a no no Momma. "

I told Quincy that I wished I could just have married him because I knew we would have been a happy, successful, bomb ass couple. Every time we talked, I let him know that if I had a chance to do things over, I would have chosen him. He would always say the same thing, "I know baby girl, shit was just complicated at the time and you had your kids to think about, one day I'm coming to scoop yo ass up tho. Until then, stop giving away that fat kat, making them niggas go crazy over yo ass."

27

I had been running around like a ho with a pimp, fucking different dudes to fill a void that would never become full because I was not with the person I truly loved and wanted. I was stuck in my sexless marriage just going through the motions of being a successful and a happy wife. Shit had to change and fast!! I was grateful to have Quincy to talk to, but I wanted to really work on getting myself back to who I used to be before I became addicted to sex.

"Alright papi, I hear everything you've said, and I completely agree with you, thank you for always telling me like it is. I just got home, and I have to make sure I get my babies fed. I love you and I'll talk to you later; you have a great day ok."

He replied, "Alright Momma, you be good shawty, I love yo ugly ass too stank butt. Hit me up when you're by yourself k.

I told him okay and hung the phone up before I stepped out of my car.

I looked up at the front of my home and thought about how blessed I was to have a family to go home to. I felt blessed beyond measure and I knew I had to get my life in order before shit hit the fan!

Chapter 9

"Amari, Darion, Maddie I'm home!" I yelled out as I entered the door. They all came running down the stairs to me with their arms open. "No No No go pick your things up off the floor and get your showers, y'all smell like you've been at a field house all day. But how was school babies?" I had to come up with something, fast, to keep my babies from touching me. I was really the one that needed to immediately jump in the shower after the type of sex I just had! My baby girl quickly interrupted my thoughts, "It was okay Mama, the kids are dumb, and the teacher let them kids just sit there and disrespect them. I would never want to be a teacher because I would knock one of them kids out!" Maddie was my 10-year-old Gemini and you just never knew which side you were gonna get from day to day. One moment she was sweet as a piece of pecan pie and the next, well, she definitely didn't have a problem telling you when she didn't want to be bothered and like it was. My 12-year-old twins, Amari and Darion were sitting in the bar stools putting the schools supplies back in their backpacks because they had fallen out when they threw the shit on my floor being careless. Amari interrupted Maddie, "Mama, I hate that school; the teachers get on my nerves and are disrespectful too. Can I just go to public school? Grandma said that I can use her address. Please Mama let me go!"

I was too tired to go back and forth with her about how she was going to stay where she was, right along with her brother and sister!

"Baby I know you don't like that school but your gonna see it through. I ain't raising quitters so get over it. Go in there, mind your business, do your work and make it back home to your Mama who loves you best. Now hurry up and do your homework, take your baths and get ready to eat. Dinner will be ready in two hours."

I quickly went into the kitchen and fixed some baked spaghetti, a chef salad e and some garlic bread. I had previously cooked the meat and noodles so all I had to do was throw everything together and put it in the oven.

By the time the food was done, my kids had done everything I had told them to do and I had managed to take that shower I needed as well.

I fixed their plates and looked up at the clock, it was 6 o'clock and my husband had still not made it home. It was so not like him to stay out that late without calling so it was alarming to the kids as well. "Mama, where's my Dad. Did he call you and tell you that he was going to be late?" My son asked with a worried tone of voice.

"Yes baby, he called and told me that he would be late, I lied. Get your plate and eat your food, make sure you three wash the dishes when you're finished."

I fixed my plate and took it up the stairs to my room. As soon as I got inside, I dialed my husband's number. He didn't answer and it pissed me off. I quickly called him right back and on the third ring he picked up. "Hey baby, I'm sorry I'm running late getting home. Shit been crazy down here, but I'll be home soon." Before I could utter a word, he hung up. I was livid, how could he be so dismissive toward me. He didn't even care what I had to say he just hung up the phone before I could say one word. That was the most disrespectful passive aggressive thing you could do to someone. I didn't want to stay up all night talking to the brick wall in the form of my husband so when he got home, 5 hours later, I was in the bed sound asleep. His entry startled me and woke me up.

Hey Baby, I'm sorry I'm coming home this late, it won't happen again." He was taking off his clothes to get in the shower. I looked my husband dead in the eyes and replied, "It's okay baby, shit happens, you're late today and I could be late tomorrow. As long as one of us are at home making sure these babies are taken care of while the other one is out, you know, handling business and being late. That's all that matters to me. Now you go and enjoy your shower, I enjoyed mine earlier, love ya...good night!". He stood there for five minutes staring at me; he was puzzled. For all he knew, I was his committed wife who gave everything I had to him and our family. I took care of him when he had nothing, I supported his dreams, and I stroked his ego when he would get down and out. I paid for him to start his business and even did most of the leg work to get it running. Every time he wanted sex, I made myself available to him. He would tell everyone every chance he got that he had the best woman in the world. Everything was perfect until one day it wasn't. He changed, he started pushing me away. His distance happened so often that it brought the ram out of me! I was so used to my husband's attention that when he stopped giving it to me, I sought it from other men.

Chapter 10

*H*ey *what are you up to lady*, I checked my phone and it was a text message from Jerome.

I'm just sitting on my deck Jerome, thinking friend. I responded

Call me lady, you sound like you have a lot on your mind.

Before I could call him, he had called me!

"Tina, I know you like the back of my hand, what's going on with you and what do you need to tell me?"

I knew that he was absolutely correct and now was the time to let him know that I had been sleeping with his child, I knew that he had never judge me in the past but this was on a whole new level! I let him know that I didn't want him to be mad at me and cut our friendship off.

"Listen, I've been fucking Kelton, like we fuck fuck friend."

He bolted out, "I knew it! I knew it that day I walked up on y'all on the aisle, the look on your face told me! That's my son, just like I know you, I know him too. Him calling you bih, that's the young dumb shit he does when he really like a girl. I got into his ass about it still because that ain't the setting to do no shit like that for one and for two, grown men don't act like that. You an Aries baby so I know how you get down. You fucked me too good in that office, I knew all that wasn't meant for just me! You were proving a point and to be honest, I ain't mad at ya! I respect you now like I've always have Tina. We were friends before any sex took place, you are a great ass honest ass person and I love you for that. You telling me this just validate everything that I've ever felt about you. You didn't have to say shit to me, and I can't be mad because we've been fucking for years now. You didn't know I had a son because my wife just found out about him too. You didn't know and I would never hold that against you, I'm sure the hell not the one who can judge anybody...haha. "

As I wept on the phone, he continued.

"Listen you will always be my friend and I will never ever judge you and you should know that by now. Now I'm gonna always keep it real with you now, that's my son so I know him better than anyone else besides his mother. However, you gotta be careful because he's a young nigga, don't get caught up! You can't be running around taking to him crazy cause he ain't got shit to lose but you do. He could be fucking you so he can tell his homeboys that he is bussing you down. Now I'm not saying he would do that but he young and dumb right now baby girl and just know when it's over, it's over, you can't be running behind him. I just want you to be aware of what you're getting yourself into. Knowing you, you're not gonna stop right now, you gotta get it out of your system and shit. Just know that I'm gonna always be here for you and I still want yo ass every chance I get shid!"

I appreciated Jerome in so many ways, his understanding and advice meant everything to me on this day. A part of me wanted to meet up with him and suck his soul out through his dick! The other part of me wanted to cry on his shoulder all night. Either way I wanted to show him how thankful I was for his compassion and understanding. As much as I wanted to give into Jerome's wish and rock his world, the other part of me never wanted to touch him again. I had made up my mind to no longer be daddy and son's pass around pussy. I was gonna fuck Kelton until I was done with his ass. I had to get wanting him out of my system!

Chapter 11

"If this funky bitch walks past us again and roll her eyes at me, I know something is up!" I leaned over and told my work BFF Sarah.

"Biiiitch, that bitch got the nerve to be walking around smelling like pudsey with a bad ass attitude. She got me fucked up! That's it, I'm finna go kick her ass! I'll whoop that white bitch's ass" Sarah stated before she started walking toward Krista. I grabbed her by the arm so fast cause she didn't play about people fucking with me and fighting was a sport for her. So, every time she got a chance, she was knocking hoes heads off their shoulders.

"Sarah, you're white, now let's get our asses up to the front before my ass get sued." We both fell out laughing. That was my roll dog, and I couldn't picture not working with her. We were Bunny and Clydette and everyone knew it too. I had moved her up to be my assistant because like myself, she was often over-qualified and overlooked because we were not part of the popular crew at the other company. I was so determined to help everyone out who had been overlooked over the years, I personally took the associates under my wings and mentored them. In one year, alone Sarah and myself made over 35 million dollars in sales. I'll never forget that year, not only did we create an unbreakable bond, she also let me know she had a strong desire to be with a black man. She was my girl so it became my mission to hook her up. I introduced her to fine ass Jamir and fireworks instantly sparked.

The introduction had happened over 5 years ago, but Jamir had turn Sarah out, so they were still hot and heavy!

"Bitch, let's get in yo office so I can tell you what Jamir done did to my ass last night, bitch my ass so sore I can barely walk straight!"

I looked at Sarah and instantly started cracking up laughing at her. It almost seemed like she had forgotten my first name and replaced it with bitch, she was the only person that could get away with that shit tho.

"Close the door behind you, girl." I told her.

As soon as the door clicked, the words fumbled out her mouth. "Jamir fucked the shit out of me so good, ooohhh, I love that mutherfuker. So, I hit him up last night after my baby's baseball game, you know I've been trying to be good and not have sex seven days a week. So anyway, he told me to come over to his house, now I had told myself that I was not leaving my house. My dumb ass put my shoes back on, bitch

37

I flew to that car and was at his house so quick. I think I got whiplashed! So anyways, I walked in his house after he opened the door and sat my ass on the couch. The whole time now I'm telling myself, Sarah, don't give up the coochie. Girl he didn't even have words for me. He walked up to me, pulled his pants down, and stuck his dick in my face. He told me open yo mouth. I didn't have time to think, I just opened my mouth and started sucking. Bitch you know I ain't as good as yo ass, but I was trying to remember to do some of yo lil tricks. I went to town on that ass and Gurl! I made his ass squeal.

Do you know this man pulled me up by my hair, snatched my shorts down, tore my shirt off of me, picked my fat ass up, carried me to his balcony and fucked the living hell out of me outside bitch? He sat me on his dick and told me to not go all the way down on it. Then he took two of his fingers and stuck them in my asshole. Bitch I ain't never had nothing in my ass but shit! I was so uncomfortable and scared at the same time cause my ass was trying to balance myself on the top ramp. I thought I was about to die! He saw me struggling so he told me to get down and he had me kneel in a chair facing it. Please tell me why he took my ass cheeks and spread them apart with his hands. He stuck his dick in me and pounded the fuck out of me for what seemed like twenty minutes straight. When he was about to nut, he snatched me around and came all over my face and in my hair. His dick was still hard, so he stuck it back in my mouth. I guess the faces I made concerned his ass, so he stopped and asked me what was wrong. I couldn't even talk my knees were on fire and I had cum all in my eyes and shit. I'm white so you know they were red, and they were bleeding. My knees were too sore to jump up and beat his ass. He had to carry me to the bathroom and wash me off, I was sore everywhere. I was so embarrassed...I know the neighbors saw us, bitch we might be on YouTube and World Star right now. I don't even know what to think about that, I felt pain and pleasure all at once. What am I going to do now? "

Before I could answer, we were paged to the customer service desk for a customer issue.

Chapter 12

As soon as I got home I kicked my shoes off and went upstairs to check on my babies. My son was at football practice and the girls were busy in their piano lessons with the instructor I had hired for them.

I made sure everything was going smoothly and that they didn't need anything from me, then I went into my room and locked the door. I didn't want to be seen having the emotional breakdown that was brewing. Out of nowhere I was overwhelmed with grief. I could not believe that I had gotten myself into an unhappy, miserable, boring ass marriage. I was sharing my body with multiple men while sharing a bed every night with a man that only wanted to cuddle. Fucking cuddle! I was disgusted because I had not been anything but an amazing wife to him up until he decided to fuck up. Before he became a millionaire with my help, he was lying and stealing from my bank accounts every chance he got. He was the best pathological liar I had ever come across. He would look me dead in the eyes and lie to my face every chance he got. I stayed with him because I'd found out that he had an alcohol addiction and I felt sorry for his ass. I associated his bullshit ways and his shortcomings with his addiction. Once I got him some help and did my part to make him successful, I'd hoped that he was a changed man and those ways were out the window. My down ass girlfriends helped me get through those tough times. Although I had some amazing friends that I could tell anything to, there were moments I felt extremely judged by some of them. I didn't want to call anyone, I wanted to cry it out and make a plan. I wanted to deal with it all alone. I knew that it wasn't typical of me to do the things I had been doing and I was wise enough to know that I was simply acting out and searching for what I wanted my husband to give me in other men. I was angry because my husband was always unwilling to listen to me whenever I tried to have a conversation with him about how I was feeling. He was distant, stubborn, and defensive. I felt that it was better to go tell another man about my issues because they would understand me before he would. I could cry on their shoulders and then get my brains fucked out. After we were done, I could go home and be the perfect wife to my sweet but stupid ass husband. I asked myself, how could someone who refused to validate my feelings and who refused to be romantically involved with his wife really love her. What the hell did he expect me to do, was it his plan to push me away to the point where I felt forced to sleep with other men so he wouldn't have to pay me alimony. I regretted ever choosing him over Quincy. I regretted choosing him over the love of my life. I hated him for destroying our marriage and being too ignorant to man up and right his wrongs. Every time I got to the point of wanting to change my ways, anger and revenge creeped up in me. I wanted to get him back. I wanted him to hurt just as much as he hurt me! He would always say that he has never cheated on me but little shit that I would come across in his phone had me thinking that was just another lie. Fuck him was my next thought, I picked up my phone and hit Quincy big dick having ass up!

"Hey Papi chulo, what are you up too?"

"Shidddd, nothing Momma. I need yo ass to come sit on my face." He replied

And just like that, he had my pussy wetter than anyone had ever made it. I got up, showered, put on my good girl perfume and went to check on the kids again. They were really focused and wanted me to stop treating them like babies. My girls had two more hours before their class was over and my son was catching a ride home with his friend so that gave me enough time to hook up with Quincy and get back home. I didn't give a damn what time my husband was coming home; he'd see me when he saw me! I told them that I needed to run off and that I would be back in a couple of hours, then out the door I went. I had missed that negro and I was going to put it on his black ass!

Chapter 13

"Momma, so you've been missing me and shit, huh?" Quincy teased as soon as I walked into his home. I didn't have to reply to him because I knew that he already knew what was up. The only thing I wanted to know was where his girl was at. He assured me that she had went back home which was in Texas, so we didn't have to worry about her interrupting us. I guess that he could sense that I needed him inside of me before we continued to discuss anything else, so he grabbed my hand and lead me to his bedroom.

"I've been missing yo fat booty ass babe." He said while he started gently taking my clothes off of me and kissing every inch of my body. I had nothing to say back, I had told him a million times how much I missed and cared for him, so he just let me take in the moment. After he undressed me, he pulled his basketball shorts off and laid on the bed, he then told me to sit on his face. I did. Quincy was the best pussy eater I had ever come across! I straddled his face and popped my shit back, forth, up, and down until I had an orgasm. He made me feel so good, I let out a loud moan. After he licked me dry, I turned around and started sucking his dick like I was getting paid to do so. I wanted him to be pleasured like he was pleasuring me. I sucked and licked every inch of him then lifted up his nut sack and went straight to his g-spot. That shit drove him crazy!

"Oh my gosh baby, you keep doing that shit you're going to catch all this nut right the fuck now!" He moaned.

I looked at him and said, "I got you, give it to me and when you go soft, I can get your thing right back the fuck up." Then I licked the tip two times for his special ass and continued to rock his shit.

He lost all control and had his orgasm. Afterwards, he picked me up and tore my vagina up by pounding it. Before we both reached our second climax, I looked at him with tears in my eyes and noticed he had tears in his as well. We didn't stop, we let them be. We both said "I love you" at the same time, we kissed each other and realized that we were making love.

All that sex had us both ready to get in the shower, so we took one together.

Quincy was my baby; we didn't link up too many times because the drive to his home was far. We had too much going on but whenever we did it was the most special time I ever had. Besides my time with my kids. We laid in bed for another twenty minutes and the whole time he just stared at me. Something in the pit of my stomach told me that he wanted to tell me something but that wasn't the right time. Something told me I knew exactly what it was! Without him saying a word, I started crying, kissed him on his forehead, then I on his lips. I got up and put my clothes back on and told him that I had to go back home. As I was heading out the door, I looked back at him and told him, "*No matter what, I want you to be happy. If she does that then you need to make her your wife. Do right by her and don't ever let her be out there in these streets feeling the way I'm out here feeling. We can't be together right now and we both know that. I don't want to, and I will never try to hold you back. I love you more than any woman besides your mother. We will be together one day, God already told me that! Now is not the time as much as it hurts me to come to this conclusion. But you better let her know she better treat you right because if she doesn't you got another woman that will! I love you Quincy!*"

He just stared at me and softly replied, "*I love you too Momma!*"

Out the door I went and straight to my car, heading back to my amazing kids that were waiting on me when I got home.

Chapter 14

It had been two months since I'd had my tryst with Quincy and I'd decided to take a break from being a freak out in the streets. Trying to be loyal to Davion, which in that year, we had sex four times and dreadful is the perfect word to describe it. After four pumps he reached his climax, rolled over on his back, and started snoring to the Gods. I made sure that I was always too busy after that because who has time for that shit.

"Baby it has been a long couple of years and I want to do something special for you. I know you've been consumed with work and so have I. How does a week in Vegas sound to you? I know that's your favorite place to go!" Davion stated. He was onto something talking like that, I instantly got excited! I didn't care what trials and tribulations we were going through; I was going to have me a ball. Now I had a reason to do some shopping and call some of my girls up to find out who wanted to tag along and bring their man with us.

"Okay baby, I'm down for that but I want to bring my friends who are also coupled up so that we can make it a couple's trip. "I quickly turned around and leaped on him, smiling from ear to ear.

He nodded and I knew that idea was approved.

I immediately called my best friends Audry, Tiffani, Coco, Keara and Lexi. They were all down for the trip. We planned to go in two weeks and I was ready to have a little retail therapy the next day!

While out and about picking up a couple of items for the trip, I got a phone call from Kelton.

He was stuck on the side of the highway, he had a 3-hour tow truck wait time and was running late for work. He told me he didn't have anyone else to call because he didn't deal with many people. A voice in my head told me to hang my damn phone up, instead, I told him to send me his location.

My friend Keara and her husband happen to own a towing company so I quickly hit her up and asked her to get his car. All she knew was that I had a young coworker whose car broke down and that she needed to take it to the nearby auto body shop. That was no issue and she did. It took us both 30 minutes to get to him. I told him to get in the car with me. I'm not sure exactly what it was, I'm assuming it was the fact that I had come and saved his day. The expression on his face when he saw me let me know that I had just turned him the fuck on. "I'm calling in baby" Kelton stated. I wasn't in the mood for his shit but for some unknown reason, I gave in. As soon as my friend and his car were out of our sight, Kelton leaned over and kissed me.

"Thank you for saving my ass, I appreciate you Ma. It's been a minute since I've seen you. You've been MIA like a motherfucker." He said,

I just looked at him and didn't say a thing.

"Listen, I can tell you're mad at me and I'm sorry for how I treat you sometimes. I'm learning and I'm trying to better myself. I love you. I know I don't act like it but you be looking out for me and I respect you for that. I'm gonna make it all up to you too! "

As he rambled on and on about his fucked up ways and how he was changing to be a better man, my mind drifted away. I started thinking about all the times I came to his rescue. His engine went out in his car, I got it fixed. He was going to be late paying his rent, I voluntarily gave him the money to pay it. His money was low for the week because he had to put his kid in daycare and because I wanted to make sure he didn't stress about it, I offered to help him out. I always offered without him asking and he always refused my help initially. So, I took full responsibility but I sat still wondering if I was just his fool. Was this his plan from the beginning when he realized that I was the HBIC, how caring and giving I could be? I didn't truly know but what I did know was that if he ever thought he could use me and then treat me like shit later, he had another thing coming! He was not going to put his hands on me again, he was not getting any-more of my money, and if I saw him extra friendly with another little bitch I was permanently ending our little escapades!

Unbeknownst to him it was game on, on my end.

He brought me back out of my thoughts when he started rubbing my pussy as I started the car. He told me to drive to a hotel that was in the next city, so I proceeded to. Once we got to the Omni Hotel, he got out and went to book our room, he told me to sit in the car. That taking control shit really did something to me. After about 10 minutes, he called me and told me to come to room 604.

By the time I made it up to the room he opened the door butt booty ass naked. He pulled me in the doorway and snatched my tights down. He snatched them so hard, they ripped. Kelton picked me up and laid me on the bed. He took off every other piece of clothing I had left on and started eating my pussy like I was his breakfast, lunch, and dinner.

Chapter 15

He licked, sucked and fingered me until I had an orgasm on his face. That shit felt so good, I looked up into his eyes. He was looking back at me so innocently. He could be very mean and I was just an hour ago questioning what the fuck he had up his sleeves but his eyes spoke to me at that moment. I realized he really needed me and that he was trying his best at this thing called life. I pulled him in closer and started kissing him. He looked back up at me and said, "I really appreciate you for everything, I can't tell you enough how grateful I am for you. I apologize for putting my hands on you and I promise that shit will never happen again. You're my baby girl and I'll always respect you. You're one of the only people that believe in me and support me no matter what. I'll always love you for that. "

I looked at Kelton and told him, "No man has ever hit me other than you. That's not something I will ever get used to. If you ever hit me again, I will kill you!" He raised up a little. I continued talking "All I've ever tried to do is support you and I'm far from perfect but I don't deserve to have you whooping my ass. I will not tolerate that. You're young and I want you to live your life. I don't expect you to commit to me because I'm a married woman. However, I do expect respect, I'll never be up on another nigga in yo face. All I ask is that you don't flaunt your flings in mine. Now I'll always have your back and I love you; more than I'll ever let you know!"

I pushed him off of me, got on top of him, and started giving him a blow job until cum started oozing out his dick. I had that lil boy freaked out and I loved the feeling it gave me!

Kelton looked up at me with his eyes bucked "This shit be blowing my mind, you doing this shit to me make me wanna knock niggas head off for even looking in your direction! I know you don't believe me but I've never experienced sex like this."

I told him, "Well act fucking right and you'll continue to get your mind and dick rocked. Now I'm tired so let's take a nap."

In 5 minutes we both were knocked out. The time was 12:45pm, when I finally woke up it 4:15pm. I panicked and raced to my phone to check my missed calls. No calls...I forgot it was Saturday and the kids were with my Mom for the weekend. My husband was at work so I was good to go.

Kelton was still knocked out like I had put the pussy on him or something. I let him lay there while my mind started racing all over again. I started thinking about the day he finally lost control and put his hands on me.

I had to go out of town to make a pop up visit at my other stores in Tennessee. I made it to the store to do a walk through early so I could be done by 5 that afternoon. I wanted to get done so I could get back to the hotel to get some rest. My week had been full of traveling and work. I was exhausted. When I made it to the hotel I noticed I had 18 missed calls from Kelton. I panicked! I quickly called him hoping everything was okay. Kelton answered the phone with a nasty attitude. "Oh, so now you answer the fucking phone, probably was somewhere sucking another nigga's dick! You're a slutty hoe ass stupid bitch!"

Being the smart ass that I am I replied, "Nawl, not this time baby. Tomorrow might be a different story and you've got some nerve, when you were just up in that little ugly ass bitch face yesterday. I saw your ignorant ass, now bye, I'm tired." As soon as those words left my mouth, I heard a knock at the door. I thought to myself, FUCK!! I knew it was him because he was the only one that knew where I was staying. He was quick to pop on me at the store. I just couldn't believe he came all the way up to Tennessee. "Who is it?" I asked. I slightly opened the door, he pushed his way in. "Move yo ass out the way, you think I'm playing with you. I've been calling you all day. Got me sitting around looking fucking stupid all day. I've been here since 12 fucking noon and you didn't wanna answer your phone. You own the company; you can answer your fucking phone any time you want to. You're so damn dumb. "he sat on the bed and looked at me like he wanted to slam me into the wall then he yelled, "Close the fucking door!"

No one had ever talked to me in that manner. I was appalled and in complete disbelief. It wasn't like I knew his ass was coming up there, he had no reason to, other than tryna get some ass. Hell he was supposed to be at work. He was just doing what he wanted to do since we were having sex but I was going to have his ass written up as soon as he got back I thought to myself.

I closed the door and sat next to him and said, "Boy you're tripping. No one told you to come here and you can leave with all that disrespectful shit you are talking." Without saying another word, he raised his hand and slapped the shit out of my face. He started to stand, as he stood up he grabbed me by my neck, he started punching me in my upper body area and told me that I was gonna stop playing with him before he kill me. He pushed me back and told me to shut my fucking mouth up before he gave me something to cry about. The tears started running down my sore and swollen face. I feared for my life. I always kept a gun in my purse and I made an attempt to grab it but he was quicker than me. He grabbed my purse and said "If you ever try to shoot me, you're gonna regret it. Now chill the fuck out girl, you got too much to lose, you can't make a scene in these white folk's hotel. You tripping" and just like that, he had simmered down and was calm as could be. I continued to sit on the bed when he reached over to pull me into his arms. His bipolar ass had me puzzled. I was stiff and frozen in place so he yanked me toward him. My entire body was sore. He held me for 2 hours while I cried in his arms. I didn't know what to do, something was going to be done but I just didn't know what. I knew that I couldn't and I wouldn't do anything to harm him at that moment unless I had to fight him off. I just stayed put until he wanted to have sex.

Chapter 16

"Baby please stop crying, your face is swollen and so are your eyes. You can't walk out that door like this. Man! I'm sorry I lost my shit on you dog, just stop crying okay?" Kelton said while pushing me back on the bed. My body was paralyzed. I was stiff as a cardboard box but he pushed me back anyway. "Please lay Tina, let me make this up to you because I was wrong and I can't take you doing all this crying." Tears were still falling but my body naturally did what he told me. He pulled my pants off and started performing oral sex on me. I continued to lay there with no emotions or sound. I still couldn't stop the tears from falling. I was extremely hurt and sore and I just wanted to end his life but I was powerless. After about 5 minutes in he stood up, took his clothes off and climbed on top of me. I was still lying there crying. He had his way with me until he reached his climax, he kissed me on my forehead, told me that he was sorry and would never hit me again, and then he went to sleep. This negro had to be crazy to actually fall asleep next to a woman he just physically assaulted. I knew I had to get out of there!

As soon as Kelton was deep in his sleep I grabbed my shit and ran out of that hotel room. Looking every bit like Angela Bassett in "What's Love Got To Do With It"!

I don't know how he got back home or when but I was on the first flight smoking.

I was a horrible liar so I didn't know how in the hell I was going to explain my bruises. I had to think fast. When I got back in town I decided I was going to Avis to rent me a car. I pulled out the lot right in front of a slow driving ass guy. Next thing I knew; I was being loaded into the ambulance headed to the hospital. I had some minor bruises and a concussion but the other driver was perfectly fine. I knew that he would be because he was driving too damn slow for anything serious to happen. I was in the hospital for two days then I was released. I needed that break. I had to clear my mind and I know that purposely causing a wreck is stupid as hell but it was the first thing that came to mind. While lying in my hospital bed I definitely knew that I didn't want Kelton anywhere around me.

I blocked his phone number, took 8 weeks off from work and I stayed at home the entire time. My husband kept going on and on about my face and how bad my body was bruised. I just laid in bed that first couple of days taking it all in and playing the victim. It was the most attention I had gotten in a long time from him. Only if he knew. When he went away, I would lay in the bed and cry because hatred had formed in my heart for all men. I would lay up wondering why life had to be so complicated. It was all my fault and I had to take responsibility for my actions, that would be my next thought, and then I would cry some more. I slipped into a depression and I wanted to give up on life. The only thing that kept me from taking my life was the fact that I did not want to leave my babies. They saved me and they didn't even know it. They knew that their mother was hurt and sometimes appeared sad, they just thought it had everything to do with the wreck. They would come in after school everyday to make sure I had eaten for the day. My oldest daughter combed my hair every week and I was hugged more in that timeframe than they had hugged me in their lifetime. I was able to cut myself off from the world and work on loving myself again.

I was scared to go back to work because I did know what Kelton would do, I knew what he was capable of. I wanted to vanish forever but that was my company and if anyone was going to stay, it had to be me. I wanted to walk in there when I got back and simply have him terminated. I was afraid so I called his father. I knew if anyone could handle him, it would be him.

"Jerome, hello is me Tina."

"Oh my God Tina, are you fucking okay! I've been worried about yo ass so fucking bad. Everyone at the job is worried about you! Do you need me to do something?" He replied.

"I'm a lot better thank you for asking. Listen I called you because I have something important to talk to you about, this is-"I was interrupted.

"I'm sorry to cut you off, Kelton is right here, he wants to talk to you!" Jerome stated.

I fucking froze and was taking a back.

"Hey, um hey Tina. I've been trying to check on you. We've been worried sick about you. How are you feeling, lady?"

Words started flying out of my mouth unfiltered!

"You have some fucking nerves getting on this phone trying to act like you are not the cause of this shit! You put your hands on me like I was a whore on the street and you were my pimp. How could you beat me of all people? I knew that you had an anger problem but never would I have thought you would have done me the way that you did. I had been at work all fucking day working my ass off, exhausted and I finally get back to my room thinking I was about to get some rest. Then you come in like a bat out of hell and you beat me! You accused me of some bullshit that was pulled straight from your ass. That's why I'm fucking your farther! And let's get one thing clear, the only man I owe an explanation about anything I do is my husband. You can't afford that title BITCH. Fuck you Kelton, I hate you and you better stay the fuck away from me or I will put a bullet in your skull and don't you even think about coming back to work because you're no longer employed by me. Find somebody else's life to fuck up because you and I are the fuck over. "

"Tina, what the fuck! What the fuck did I just hear you say? Kelton hit you? Oh my God! Are you fucking kidding me!" Jerome chimed in. He had the phone on speaker and I didn't know it. I was glad because I knew that I didn't have the strength to call him back after I cursed Kelton's ass out. I was just going to hang up and block his number too. Before I could respond I started to hear Jerome and Kelton start fighting. The call dropped and I just put my phone down. I could care less what the hell was going on over there. I cut my phone off and started watching " Evil lives here" on the ID Channel.

Chapter 17

All hell broke loose between them two, Kelton was beyond pissed to find out that I had slept with Jerome. Jerome was pissed that his son had the nerve to actually put his hand on a woman. I had heard rumors that he was very disrespectful to the mother of his child but never anything alarming like he would hit her. Neither one of them knew where I lived to my knowledge so I was shocked when Jerome showed up to the security office of my gated community one afternoon. No call, no warning! Thank God Davion had to go out of town for a couple of days on a business trip. The lead security office called to make sure it was okay for him to allow Jerome in. He had never made me feel like he would harm me and I was in a better mood that day so I approved his entrance.

Once he made it to my front porch I had mustered up enough energy to meet him at my front door.

Jerome looked like he had been through pure hell. I told him to come in and have a seat on the sofa.

"Jerome I'm going to let you say whatever you have to say and then I'll respond. Just please don't do anything to make me feel like you are going to hurt me because I'm going to shoot your ass if you do." I calmly said.

He looked at me in disbelief.

"Tina, I would never do anything to you baby and I'm so sorry that my son did. I just needed to talk to you because shit has hit the fan at home. Kelton is my child and I love him, always will but I had to lay his ass out! "

My heart started racing because I instantly started worrying about Kelton and if he was okay. I mean I knew that he wasn't dead because Jerome wouldn't have been at my house if that was the case! "First, let me start off by saying, I can't believe you told him about us! What the fuck Tina? His ass went crazy and I had to quickly react. I swung on him before I could gather my thoughts. That lil nigga had the nerve to punch the shit out of me right back. I can't believe that my own child would swing on me. I had to fight my own child over a female. My wife walked in on us and broke it up. Kelly was looking at us like we were crazy. She wanted to know what was going on and why in the hell were we fighting like two niggas in the street. I didn't even know what to tell her, I couldn't fucking gather my thoughts Tina! I just knew that if I told the truth, she'd kill my ass. I had to get the hell out of there, quick! "

I stopped him because dealing with everything that he was telling me was overwhelming. I did not wake up thinking I was going to have to deal with that shit. I wanted him, his son, and our previous sex encounters to be nonexistent in my life at that moment but it was too late and I had to deal with the problem that I was partly a part of and find a resolution. I told Jerome that I was going to call Kelton and try to get him to hear me out. I didn't want him at odds with his son and vice versa. I unblocked Kelton and dialed his number. He picked up on the first ring. "Man, baby how could you sleep with my Pops, you fucked my fucking daddy my nigga. I guess you'll fuck me then go give him some ass, huh? That's some cold shit."

I stopped him dead in his tracks. I let him know that I had sex with his father before him and before I knew of his existence.

"Listen, I have only been with him three times and like I said, that shit was before you. I didn't say anything because we have an understanding and you know this. You do you; I do me, no questions asked. I would not and have never done you dirty. I wouldn't do no shit like that! I love your father and I love you too. Even though you treat me crazy and just physically abused me, I still want the best for you. You need to make this shit right with your father, pronto. Y'all need to meet up and squash all of this because fighting over me ain't

63

it and after that's done, take your crazy ass to some anger management classes. I hung up after that; looked at Jerome, and told him to call his child, I told him that I was sorry and that I was going to need a little space and time to process everything that had occurred. I wanted him out of my damn house. I was tired and ready for them both to leave me the hell alone. Jerome pulled out his phone, called his child, and told him to meet him at the center he worked at. He thanked me, got up and headed to the door. Before he fully made his way out he looked back at me and said, "you look sexy as fuck right now Tina, let me put the tip in real quick. Please, I won't tell. After all, I had the pussy first."

I gave him the nastiest look that I could muster up. Words were not needed. I was appalled that he had the nerve to say that after everything that went on. He took his ass right out my door and I locked it behind him. I was never fucking him again!

Chapter 18

I was laying in the bed watching TV when I heard my husband come up the stairs and go into our youngest daughter Maddie's bedroom. As soon as he stepped in I heard her ask him who was that man that was over here earlier talking to her Mama. Those damn children of mine were nosy and they talked too much. I thought that they were up stairs on the phone with their cousins not paying me any attention. I knew his ass was gonna fly into my room questioning me next and that's just what he did. As soon as he walked in the door I had a lie waiting for his ass. I told him that the man who came earlier wanted me to sponsor a fundraiser event for one of his boys and girls club locations. Not too much but just enough to get him out of my face. At this point I was over men and particularly my husband. All he could do was shut the fuck up talking to me and let me be. He did just that and he never brought it up again.

I came back to reality when Kelton moaned, "You alright ma? I love you okay! "

I looked over at him and told him that it was time for us to get ready to go. I had been there doing freaky things to that man long enough and I was ready to get home to my babies. Plus, I wanted to get on the phone with my home-girl Audry and gossip about any and everything. Kelton looked at me and asked if he would ever see me again. I knew if I told him no, that I would be lying so I just told him the truth rudely. Yeah yo ass will if you behave now get the fuck up and get yo shit on so we can go nigga.

He stood up butt naked and his dick was still rock hard. I thought to myself, why does his dick gotta be so damn big, damn what are these dudes made out of! He saw me looking straight at his erection and walked over to me. There was no denying it, that thing had some power over me. Next thing I knew; we were fucking again. This time we both pleased each other with intense energy the entire time. At that moment we had a connection like never before. At that moment of ecstasy, I realized that I loved his young ass. After we both finished he pulled me in, kissed my lips over and over, then looked me in my eyes and said, "I'm in love with you Tina." I just stared back at him then told him that we were solid. I hugged him tighter and he knew the feeling was mutual. No additional words were needed. After another hour we were finally ready to walk out of the door.

I had been off of work and cupped up in my home not talking to anyone but close family and friends for over a month so I didn't know anything about what anyone had going on. That included him. I had to ask him where he wanted me to take him. Apparently things were too awkward between him and his Pops so he had moved to another apartment complex near the city to put some distance between them. He asked me to drop him off there. We pulled up to the front entry and I was highly impressed and puzzled at the same time. He was living in a gated apartment complex but I realized it was literally 5 minutes away from my gated community. I loved his ass but being so close to my family was something I didn't want. He was too unpredictable for that shit. I wasn't sure if he knew where I lived but I knew if his Pops found me and he could too. My heart started racing but I didn't say a thing. I gave him a kiss good night and let him go on his way.

On my way home I started feeling light headed and I attributed that to finding out that my world could really be flipped upside down if something popped off between Kelton and I again. I knew that he wouldn't hesitate to come show his ass at any given moment.

I got home and called my home-girl Tiffani to see if she was packed and ready to go on the Vegas trip. I knew the answer before I asked because Tiff was that friend that you knew was gonna have your back in any situation on vacation and she was always ready to hop on a plane. Every time I went out of town I wanted Tiffani to go. Hell, if she was there with me when Kelton popped up, that situation would have never happened like that.

As she was going over our itinerary for the trip I felt myself feeling nauseous. I quickly told her to hold that thought, I threw the phone down and ran to my master bathroom. I couldn't remember eating anything because I was too busy fucking Kelton's brains out to be hungry. Maybe that was the problem I thought. I went back to the phone and told Tiffani I hadn't eaten all day so I was going to go make me a tuna sandwich. As soon as I opened the can of tuna I immediately told her that I would call her back later because I wasn't feeling well. I threw the can down on the counter and I had to run to the guest bathroom. This time I didn't make it, puke was everywhere. The smell of tuna made me nauseous all over again. After having two pregnancies I knew what was up, my ass was pregnant and all hell was about to hit the fan if the baby was not my husband's.

Chapter 19

What happens in Vegas stays in Vegas and we had a great time living the high end lifestyle. We parted with the celebrities, went to concerts, dined at up scaled restaurants and gambled into the wee hours of the night. I enjoyed spending quality time with my girlfriends while the guys went to strip clubs and parties. I was a full time mother, workaholic, and sexaholic. I hardly made time for vacations anymore so it was well needed and I took full advantage of the time. Everything was perfect except the fact that certain smells made me sick as hell. By the end of the trip everyone knew that I was with child!

"Baby you're pregnant and you gotta go to the doctor as soon as we get back home. You've been out of work and I messed around and put something in ya!" my husband proudly said.

He was so damn full of delusion I couldn't believe it.

As soon as we arrived home I made a doctor appointment to find out how far along I was. That was important because that will tell me who could and who couldn't be the father. I made sure to book the appointment when Davion was going to be tied up at work. When the doctor told me that I was already 16 weeks alone, I was so glad that he was not in that room with me!

I instantly knew that there was no way my husband was my baby's father. It was either Quincy or Kelton and I didn't know how I was going to clean up this mess. This was the beginning of the end for my perfect life as everyone one else saw it.

"Hey baby, I just left the doctor's office and we're six weeks. Because of all the trauma. I've been through I will be considered a high risk pregnancy. If I don't take it easy I could have the baby very early. My intuition is telling me I've really have to work lightly but you know that's going to be extremely challenging." I was going to build a lie so good everyone was going to fall for it. The only challenge I would have is keeping him away from all my doctor's appointments.

I could not tell him this baby was not his because I knew he would be devastated and so would my kids. Besides that, divorces could get nasty I never wanted to be that person in and out of court rooms fighting over assets. Yeah I wasn't telling him shit. And just to be on the safe side, I hired a private investigator to follow him so that I could compile as much dirt on him as possible just to have in my back pocket. If divorce was what our relationship had to come down to, I was going out swing! Davion simply replied, "Don't you let anything happen to my baby and I can't ever imagine living without you Tina. We're rich now so you don't have to go back to work. But, I know how you are and I'm certain that you will insist on going regardless of what I say. Just take it easy baby." I told him our life was more important than any company and that I planned on taking things lightly but I was most definitely not becoming a stay at home mother.

I decided to go back to work two weeks after my doctor's visit and by that time my pregnancy was slightly visible. It looked like I had been off eating one too many cookies out of the cookie jar. As soon as I entered my front office Sarah ran in and closed the door.

"Bitch, I've missed you so fucking much! You better not ever leave me like that again, I mean got damn you've been gone for a whole century bitch!" I stopped Sarah in mid-sentence, "Kelton jumped on me, in anger I let it slip that I fucked Jerome and now I'm pregnant and it's either Quincy's or Kelton's." Her rosy toned face instantly turned white. The information I had just given her came like a nuclear bomb. Sarah's mouth flew up and all I heard was noooo biiiitch. The waters I had gotten myself in were muddy and I couldn't believe it myself. A part of me wanted to cry and the other half wanted to laugh because of the look Sarah was giving me.

She asked me what I was going to do and I let her know my plan. I told her that she would be my ally. If I called her for anything at any time she had to be ready to tell a lie quicker than a cat could lick his ass. I knew she had my back and would never tell anyone so I had no worries.

Our conversation was interrupted by a knock on the door. It was a cashier that had a question concerning her register. Sarah gave her the information she needed and she excused herself back out of the office. We were so wrapped up with the information I had just given her that we didn't notice the door was cracked open. I proceeded to tell her how I was in so much disbelief about the possibility of having Kelton's baby. As soon as those words left my mouth Kelton's voice interrupted, "So when were you gonna tell me that you're carrying my child?"

Chapter 20

It was like all the oxygen had gotten sucked out of the room! Oh fuck! I thought, as I looked up and saw his confused looking face. I didn't want him to blow up in the store so I asked him to come in and have a seat. I looked at Sarah and told her to stay with me and make sure she locked the door. I knew that if he tried anything he'd have to go through her first and he wasn't the type to let everyone know his business so he would keep his cool. He had no idea that she already knew everything it was to know about him including his dick size. Most of the time I shared too much with her, I'd have to kill her if we ever fell out because she knew too much of my dirt!

Kelton would not take his eyes off of me and before I could say anything, he asked "Why is she in here?" She replied, "I'm in here cause I'm in here", sitting up in her chair to prove her point. My response was simply, "You know why!" He said nothing else about her presence.

I told him that I didn't know how I was going to explain the situation to him so I was asking Sarah what I should do. I let him know that my life was about to change and that I was terrified because I didn't know how my husband was going to react. Half of that was the truth, the other part was bullshit. I wasn't going to tell him a damn thing. Kelton's facial expression went from somewhat angry and confused to concerned.

"Do you think he gone try to fuck with you cause I'll beat his fucking ass about you!" Kelton said while leaning in toward me. I stopped him in his tracks and reminded him that he is the father of my kids and I would never want anything to happen to any man I've ever been with. I told him that you never know what someone will do in the heat of the moment but I wanted to make sure me and the kids would be safe, more than anything. He nodded his head in agreement and leaned back in his sit. I was reassured that myself and my babies would be just fine because all I needed was his help to take care of this baby we created. I don't know if it was my pregnancy hormones or the fact that I was extremely emotional exhausted but I started crying my eyes out. Kelton leaped out of his seat and hugged me tighter than he ever had. He pulled my face up toward his and told me, "Man! don't cry, I got you and my baby. I'm going to step up and be the man you need me to be and that's for life baby girl". Without thought, I pulled him closer to me and started French kissing him. We were so focused on tonguing each other down we forgot all about Sarah's ass being there loving every bit of that moment. She wanted to slap him into a coma but just like every other woman that got one glimpse of him, she thought he was one of the finest man she had ever laid eyes on.

She would always tell me that I never had to worry about her being inappropriate with him but looking at him could never hurt anyone. I was okay with that because he was just like an expensive art piece in human form.

She startled us when she coughed loudly and said "I mean damn, just take ya'll clothes off already!" Kelton started smiling and told me he had to get back on the floor.

As soon as he walked out the door Sarah looked at me and said, "bitch what we gonna do about Quincy because you know I will be quick to call him because he has always been my favorite. "I told her not to involve herself when it came to him. I instantly became overwhelmed with how I was going to figure shit out and in a hurry because all these niggas were about to be fighting. Sarah looked at me and burst out into laughter. She looked up to me with a silly grin and said, "Now you got me scared. I wanted another baby but I don't know who the daddy will be because your ass has been with everybody in town, making them fall in love and shit! "That's when I proceeded to try to beat her ass but she ran out of the office. I could never take her seriously. That girl was damn crazy but I love her because I needed that laugh.

After I spent thirteen totaled hours catching up on the business, having manager meetings, and conducting two conference calls. I decided to head to my Grandmother's house to check on her. It had been a couple of months since I had seen her face to face so I wanted to stop by and spend some quality time with her.

I arrived at her home and let myself in with the key I had made ten years ago. As soon as the door opened I heard my Grandmother's voice say, "Come on in baby, God got a message for you." My heart drop!

Chapter 21

"Tina Marie! You're going 120 on a 45 mph road baby. One or two things are going to happen, you're going to get pulled over and get a ticket or you're more than likely going to crash and get someone killed. He hasn't shown me exactly what you got going on but I know that you've been dancing with the devil shuga . Stop your shit and fix the mess you're in,"

I told her yes Granny and walked in the kitchen to fix her something to eat. I did not want to explain to her what all was going on because I was too embarrassed. I was not raised to do the things I was doing. Fuck living on the wild side, it was too crazy even for me. A spent two hours with my Grandma and then I was ready to go home. I started feeling sick and needed to rest my body. This baby was kicking my ass. Before I left I turned around and told my Grandma that I loved and appreciated her and she responded with congratulations. She helped my single teen mother raise me and we were two peas in a pod. Most of the time only a few words were needed to have a full conversation. I understood at that moment that she knew that I was with child; so I thanked her, gave her a kiss on the cheek and left.

As soon as I pulled onto the street leading to my house, I received a phone call from the private investigator I had hired to find out what the fuck my husband had been up to.

"Mrs. Tina Fowler, sorry to interrupt you so late but I would like to meet up with you to go over some of my findings. Are you available at the moment?"

That's my saving grace! I thought.

"Sure, sure, sure, can you meet me at my store? I can turn around and head back there. "

He agreed to meet me there in 10 minutes, by the time I arrived he did as well. The store was closed which was perfect because I did not want anyone to disturb, distract, or over hear our conversation!

A million things were running through my head but the most important thing was my kids. I didn't know how they would handle not having two parents in the same house. Things had gotten so awkward for me. Finding out that my husband was running around on me was something I was not going to settle for. One would think that I had no right to feel this way when I've been doing the same thing but it did I don't give a damn. He hurt me with his distance. He pushed me away for years before I had my first affair. I felt he should have been a man and corrected his wrongs. He should have fixed his relationship with me and did everything to assure me that he wanted to support me, sexually be attentive, and validate my feelings. He didn't and he took the coward's way out, he deflected and played the victim. I hated him and I despised him for that. I could not understand how a man, who had the world at his fingertips, a life most can only dream of, a wife that adored and did everything to show her love for him, and beautiful kids that worshipped the grounds Daddy walked on could be so neglectful and stupid. He was a stupid simple minded son of a bitch to me. Every tear he made me cry, every pain I felt, I wanted his ass to feel.

Corner, the investigator quickly snapped me out of my thoughts. He let me know that I needed to brace myself because he had gathered a lot of information. He let me know that he hated to give me this type of information this late at night but this was the time it needed to happen. My heart started beating heavily because I surely didn't want to get so upset that I'd end up going home and kill the man with my bare hands. I had to tell myself to brace up and get prepared to handle my business like the G I had always been. I told him to let me have it and that's just what he did.

Chapter 22

"Well like I said, I hate to be the bearer of bad news and there is simply no other way to put it. Your husband is indeed having an affair with another woman. In fact, he also has two kids with her." Corner said. There was a part of me that knew in the pit of my gut that he had been seeing someone else. The fact that he actually had not one, but two kids is what got me!

Here I am worried about letting him know that I was having an outside child and his ass had already beat me to the punch times two! I was livid but I was going to play my cards right and let his ass have it. I was so caught up in my thoughts that I didn't focus on what Corner said next until he pulled some pictures out and slid them in front of me. I was floored when I saw who was in them. It was my bald headed, hoe ass cousin Chantelle. My husband had been cheating on me with my cousin.

I sat there looking at the pictures; hoping that somehow my own eyes were playing tricks on me but no; the pictures were actually in front of me; they were there. My no-good lying husband and my cousin who had slept with half the town. Her own mother had put her out of the house at 14 for sleeping with her ol' man. She was the girl having sex with all the boys in the neighborhood in the back yard and shit. She even got caught letting a group of boys gang bang her in a ditch that was by the family house we grew up in. But yet, my dumb ass husband fell for her broke ass. The girl couldn't keep a job for more than 2 weeks and to add insult to injury, she had lost custody of their two daughters 2 years prior to me finding out all of this. Here he was, going all out for the irresponsible as bitch.

They would take road trips to nearby cities, shop, go to art galleries, eat out at upscale restaurants and go to different hotels to fuck. Meanwhile, I was left all alone to fill my loneliness by sleeping with other men. He had time to spend with her and introduce her ignorant ass to the finer things of life but could barely keep up a conversation with me. The icing on the cake was to know he had actually had sex with me after raw dogging her stinking ass when I know she had several transmitted diseases when we were teens. I felt every emotion there was to feel; Shock, hurt, anger, rage, revenge, and numbness, I felt it all. After hearing the private investigator give me all the details and show me every picture he had taken of them, I thanked him and let him know I had heard enough. I was ready to calmly go home, get in my bed, and call it a night. I was mentally and physically exhausted. I wasn't in the mood to run him over that night, he'd live to see another day, on me.

It was late when I pulled into my driveway, my husband's car was parked there and he had left the light on for me. When I walked in the house I smelled the stench of fried chicken. I walked in the kitchen and saw a plate left on the stove with my name on it. He had gotten home early and cooked a Sunday meal on a weekday. I slid the plate toward the trash compactor and rolled my eyes before I knew it. The nerve of that nigga to cook now. I couldn't remember the last time he tried to cook a damn thing in my house. I went upstairs and kissed my babies; they were knocked out but I didn't care. I always made sure I told them goodnight whether they could hear me or not. When I walked in the room, Davion was sitting at the computer desk, He leaped up and ran to hug me. "Hey baby where have you been, you're a little late today huh?" I looked at him and told him that I had a lot of business to handle at the store so I had to stay later. He picked me up without warning and placed me on the bed. "Baby I've been missing you, I'm so ready to spoil you this entire pregnancy. Anything you want, just let me know and it's yours." I looked at him and asked, "Anything?" Davion told me "Yes baby, anything." The words flew out of my mouth without warning, "Will you stop fucking Chantelle and making kids with her?"

Davion's black ass turned white. My words were as heavy as a ton of bricks.

"Baby, Baby, Baby, what….what are you talking about. I got up and walked to my purse, I pulled out a copy of the pictures and handed them to him. I looked at him and said, "I've had a very long and tiring day today. Your lies are not needed so spare me the bullshit. I know that you have been fucking my nasty ass cousin and I know that you've nutted in the whore and got her pregnant twice. The lie; "it was a mistake" is not needed, you trying to convince me that you love me and not her skank ass is not needed, you trying to convince me to not divorce your scandalous ass and take everything you own is not needed. I've been in this piece of shit marriage with you too long, dealing with your wack ass sex, being neglected and made to feel unworthy. Fuck you and that whore, you're lucky this baby has drained my energy and I'm not in this bitch fucking you up. So what I need you to do is take your basic ass down stairs and get out of my face before I Al Green your dumb looking ass tonight !

I got back in the bed, pulled the covers over my head and was knocked out before he knew what had hit him.

Chapter 23

I was awoken by my kids getting ready for school, I wanted to remain as calm as possible because I did not want to disrupt their day. I didn't care what their father and I was about to go through, my number one goal was to protect them and make sure their life was not interrupted as much as possible. Once they headed out the door and got on the bus, I heard Davion's footsteps coming up the stairs. Once he entered the room I noticed that he looked like shit. I could tell that he had not slept a wink all night. He had sat up all night, crying and trying to figure out how in the hell he was going to fix this situation. His expression told me that he knew he had fucked up majorly. My husband got down on his knees as said,

"Baby, it really ain't much I can say at this point, I really messed up. You don't deserve what I did to you. I have fucked up my family and I know it. I'm so sorry you had to go through this and find out about it while you are carrying my baby. Baby, I know I'm gonna sound stupid but please, I'll do anything. Please let's go to counseling and work this out. I can't lose my family. I love you and my babies, I can't handle seeing you move on and be with somebody else. We've been together since we were teens Tina. I fucked up and I don't give a damn about her stupid ass. I'm sorry Tina, please work it out with me. Please. "How could a man say he doesn't give a damn about a woman who had two of his kids, how could he allow the system to take custody of his kids. He was pathetic to me and I had lost the little respect I had left for him after finding this out. I looked at him, rolled my eyes and told him to get the fuck out of my face because we were done.

He packed a suitcase full of clothes and left the house like I asked him to, crying the entire time. Anger had set back up in me and I wanted to get even. Every man that hurt me or made me feel any negative type of way, I wanted revenge. Just like that something snapped inside of me and I was a woman scorned and on a mission.

Now that I had gotten that situation temporarily taken care of, it was time for me to handle the other guys, one by one. Jerome's ass was up next. It pissed me off that he still wanted to sleep with me after he knew that I had been having sex with his son. It bothered me that he would beg to have sex with me but after I continually turned his advances down, he started acting weird as fuck when we were around each other. It was almost as if he was salty because he knew I wasn't into him like he wanted me to be. Jerome wanted some type of love affair were we would sneak off, fuck each other's brains out, go home, text and flirt all day then continue throughout the night. That wasn't gonna happen even if I hadn't fuck Kelton's fine ass. I never had feelings for him like that. I considered him just a good friend that I would fuck every four years when I felt like it. After he found out that I had separated from my husband he started consistently pressuring me to have sex with him. Having sex with him was more of a job and less pleasure. He was cool and he was my boy but he was doing too much and I wasn't checking for him at all. He had started getting on my nerves and I had been over him. He was too fine to be chasing me when all the other ladies he came in contact with were dying to sleep with him. I guess men really do want what they can't have. Maybe he was trying to prove to himself that he still had it and there was no way he was letting his son run off with his side bitch. I really don't know what was going on in his mind but clearly his wife had her vagina on lock from his ass because he was always pressed and doing too much to get my attention!

Chapter 24

"Jerome, we need to talk, I need to come by your office after hours and just so you know, I only have ten minutes so don't be trying to fuck cause I'm not feeling it!" I got my words out quickly and hung up on his ass because I was not in the mood for his inappropriate response or bullshit.

I immediately called my home-girl Tiffani and let her know that I needed her to take me to have a serious conversation with Jerome. He had never been violent with me but I wasn't taking any chances. Tiffani was one of my closest friends and she would never judge me so I knew that I could trust her with my secrets. I gave her a full rundown of everything I had been up to with everyone and it felt good to come clean to someone without judgement. Her mood went from innocently there to support her friend to being on beast mode and ready to ride with her friend.

Tiffani reached down and picked her purse up, she opened it and pulled a 9mm out and said, "I stay ready now grab yours and let's go. We can't put nothing past these negros."

I pulled up to the front door of Jerome's office and told Tiffani to stay in the car until I called her. I don't know why I even thought to tell her that because I knew there was no way she was just gonna sit in a damn car and wait on me. She looked up at me and said, "Yeah right! I'll be in there when that little feeling in the pit of my stomach kicks it." And then she started laughing. I couldn't help but to chuckle back at her and then I proceeded to walk into the building nervously. I didn't even have a fucking game plan. I didn't know what the hell I was about to say to this man. I just knew that I was beyond tired of his shit. As I entered the door to his office I heard B.B. King's Rock Me Baby playing in the background. To my surprise, this motherfucker had the nerve to be sitting butt ass naked on his desk with a hard ass dick on go.

He looked at me with the creepiest grin ever and said, "I want that fat pussy so bad baby. Come ride this dick like only you can do it."

Before I could tell him how the only thing I would be doing was cutting him the fuck off, I heard Tiffani behind me taking pictures and starting to let his ass have it.

"You nasty married freak, my friend is tired of your extra horny cheating ass. What you won't do is keep trying to pressure her to fuck yo weird ass, what you will do is leave her alone before I tell your wife what you and yo son been up too and let's get one thing straight, you may be a friend to her but I don't give two fucks about you, yo son, yo wife, or them three ugly ass kids y'all got together. I don't mind fucking up a fake ass happy home. Come near her again and English funeral home will be coming to pick up your body.

The shocking thing is Jerome sat on the desk just as naked and calm as can be and let Tiffani say whatever she wanted without ever interrupting her.

I chimed in with a calmer demeanor, "Listen Jerome, I am so sorry but I've been uncomfortable for a minute dealing with you. I've lost so much respect for you because I simply can't understand how a man would aggressively continue to try to sleep with a woman knowing his son has also had a sexual relationship with her. You were my fine ass friend and I loved that I could always be honest with you about everything. Things have changed, they're awkward because you know that I'm pregnant. The fact of the matter is; I think I'm carrying your grandchild. I'm not 100 percent sure right now but there is a 50/50 chance that the baby is Kelton's."

Jerome went from looking me dead in the eyes with the look of confusion to dropping his head. He stood up as Tiffani and I eyes were fixated on his penis, he picked his clothes up off the chair and started putting them on. If that man didn't have anything, he had a big ass dick and I was staring and wondering how the hell did it stay hard this entire time when he began to talk.

Chapter 25

"'Tina, I can't fucking believe you baby, you could have just come to me woman to man instead of creating this fucking circus. There is no way in hell I would have ever done some shit like this to you. You got me sitting here with my nuts on display hanging, really? Honestly I trusted you, I thought that we were better than this. You really brought another person in here to curse me out and talk to me like I ain't shit?"

I cut him off and tried to explain to him that I told her to stay in the car but he wasn't trying to hear anything else from me. He looked up at me and said "You fucking with the wrong one!"

By this time, he had made it to his cabinet by his front window and pulled out his pistol. I quickly turned to look at Tiffani who had hers aimed back at him.

"Oh my God, what the hell have I gotten us into?" I thought. I didn't come here for someone to get killed. I just wanted his sexual advances to stop and to dead our affair. I became enraged and leaped at him. I completely forgot everything that mattered to me in that moment. I guess the leap caught him off guard because he dropped the gun and fell to the ground. Because I didn't have time to grab my gun, I had to go for what I knew. I kneed him in his nuts and started scratching his eye balls. That gave Tiffani enough time to make her way over to us and put the gun right up to his temple. He was in pain and didn't know what the hell we were going to do to him. He became so frightened he pissed his pants.

Every curse word I had heard came out my mouth. I saw red and started throwing Mike Tyson punches. This negro had the nerve to pull a gun out on me. I slapped his ass every time that thought ran across my mind.

"I tried to tell yo ass that I wasn't trying to have this go down like this but you didn't want to listen you stupid as mutherfucker. It didn't have to go down like this. I do not want you and I will never want you so leave me a damn lone, you son of a bitch! I hate you! I hate all y'all punk ass men and if you ever come near me again, I am gonna personal blow yo fucking brains out.

By the time we made it to the car heading toward my house I had gone into full panic attack mode. Things had gotten very intense to say the least and I became scared of his retaliation. I did not know what he would do to me but more importantly, I didn't know if my kids would be affected.

Thank God Tiffani was there to snap me out of it. She assured me that he was the one terrified because not only did we just kick his ass but, there was no way he wanted those pictures of him sitting there with a hard on to be released. She told me that from her observation of him, in some sick way it probably was a turn on. I don't know if that was a fact but what I did know was he was at his highest level of being pissed off at me. I was pretty sure that he was never showing back up to work and he would never tell a soul what had transpired so I wasn't worried about Kelton finding out or being at work. You could never put anything past anyone so just for precaution, I was going to take a couple of days off. It was time for me to take some self-defense classes and load up on some more guns!

Chapter 26

I stayed out of work for three weeks to gather myself. I had decided that I wanted to get as far away from that place and those people as I could before I did anything else stupid. Sometimes time heals wounds and I wanted to spend time alone with just the kids. I didn't tell anyone but my Granny, she would be worried if she didn't know where I was, everyone else would have to just be okay. I didn't want anyone else trying to go with me or accidentally telling someone who didn't need to know where I was. I packed my babies' luggage and went to California to let our hair down and enjoy the beach life. Just the four of us and it was the best decision I had made in the last couple of years. We enjoyed walking through Hollywood Blvd, going to TJ's Sweetie Pie's NoHo, visiting Madame Tussauds, taking the Hollywood Tour and seeing the celebrity homes located in the hills. My babies were so excited when we rode past Beyoncé, Jay Z, and Tyler Perry's homes. We enjoyed driving to San Francisco and Venice Beach as well.

Amari, Darion, and Maddie would always be worn out by the time we made it back to our room at The Beverly Hills Hotel.

As close as they were to their dad, it shocked me that he had not called one time since we had been there. What was more puzzling is that they never questioned his whereabouts.

The only person who was wondering about his dusty ass was me. He had only called me about the kids three times since he was kicked out of the house. He would always ask the same old generic ass questions like, where are the kids and what have they been up to. Then he would proceed to question and beg me to get back with him. I guess he was really only concerned about the kids he was living with. Now my babies were getting a taste of the neglect that my cousin's kids endured. Word around town was that he was seen taking his other kids shopping at the expensive outlets we use to take our kids. I cannot lie and act like hearing that information didn't hurt me because it did. That man hid two whole children and an affair behind my back and if shit didn't go down the way it did, I would have really been looking like a stupid naive wife to everyone who knew us when it finally did. Tears started falling down my cheeks as I laid in the bed thinking about it. At that moment I decided I wanted to go through the courts to establish visitation and I would never deal with his sneaking no good ass again. I fought the urge to call him and blocked his damn number on my phone. My thoughts were interrupted by a text message from Kelton. He hit me up to check on me because I had not called him and answered any of his phone calls in weeks.

I knew that he was good for hunting me down and popping up without warning and I didn't want any of that to happen so I sent him a reply. I let him know that I had to handle some business and I had a death in the family. I had become great at telling lies at this point. He began telling me how he missed me, the baby, and my sweet pussy. The more he talked the more my eyes rolled in their sockets. I made it my duty to end that conversation as quickly as it started by letting him know that I would contact him when I got back in town. I was not in the mood to hear shit else he had to say. Fuck Kelton, fuck Davion, and of course fuck Jerome!

Half way through the trip I did get a pleasant phone call from Quincy. I was so glad that it was later in the evening and my kids were settled in the beds because I craved his presence and conversations in during trying moments. His honesty and caring demeanor was always soothing to my soul. Our intense conversation always made my pussy throb too.

Chapter 27

"**M**omma" what the fuck yo fat booty ass doing huh?" I burst into laughter. He was so comical to me even when he wasn't trying to be or saying the same thing.

I replied, "I'm in LA with the kids enjoying a much needed vacation, what are you up too mister?"

He proceeded to tell me that he had to take an unexpected work trip to Cali too and that day was his off day. My heart dropped because everything in me wanted to meet him and have another round of awesome sex and great conversation to follow. I couldn't fight the urge and before I could ask him to stop by my hotel he asked me where I was. The Beverly Hills Hotel flew out of my mouth. He asked me if my husband was with me and I let him know that it was only the kids and I. He told me that he was only eight minutes away from me and assured me that he'll join me in about 20 minutes or so. I told him my room number and told him I would let the front desk clerk know that I was expecting company. We hung up and I then jumped in the shower. I wanted to be fresh and smell so good for his ass. I knew he was gonna see my belly and be like what the hell but I was preparing myself to be completely honest and forthcoming with him.

After twenty minutes I heard the doorbell ring. It was my handsome Quincy. He stepped into the living room of my suite and whispered, "where are the kids?"

I let him know they were in their room sleeping. Before I could say anything he looked down at my stomach and back up at me, wondering what the fuck was going on in my stomach. I told Quincy a lot had happened in his absence and that we needed to talk. I pulled him into my bedroom and guided him toward the bed. When he sat down I told him everything! I told him about what I had been up to, about Kelton's abusive ass, Jerome being Kelton's father and our altercation, I even told him about Davion being caught by the detective.

Quincy sat there and stared at me for all of ten minutes without uttering a word. In all my years of knowing him, I've never seen him lost for words.

I became nervous and then embarrassment set in. Maybe I should have kept all that information to myself I thought. Out of nowhere Quincy grabbed my chin and asked, so you think the baby is mine? And then he reached over, grabbed the Kleenex of the night stand, and started wiping my tears. I told him the truth, it was between him and Kelton. His hand slid down to my belly and he started rubbing it. He stood up, picked me up and put me toward the middle of the bed. I was confused because he is a talker and I had given him a lot of information about the crazy things I had been up to so there was no way he could be in the mood for sex. At that point I had lost my sexual appetite but no matter what the situations may be, we were like two magnets, we always ended up touching each other when we were close to one another. Quincy pulled my nightgown up, slid my panties off, and started eating me like he was at the Carnival Buffet! His tongue set my soul on fire. He licked, he kissed, he fingered until I reached my climax. I attempted to pleasure him orally but he stopped me and said "I don't need that tonight, I just want to satisfy you and then feel that wet pussy on my dick baby."

I undressed him, sat up on my knees and guided his fat long brown dick into my vagina. The thought of this man fucking the shit out of me made it so horny I wanted to scream. As soon as the tip went in he started losing control in a way I had never seen him do.

"Got damn baby, yo shit wet as fuck! If this ain't my baby, I'm about to put another one in you tonight!"

I started doing kegels on his dick, I love how my sex made a man lose all control. This pregnant pussy really made him go crazy! I fucked that man for the rest of the night and made him forget all about his fiancé. Fuck her, whoever she was, I had him first!

Chapter 28

Before I knew it the clock read 7:39am and I knew my kids would be bursting into my room around 8:30am. I looked over at Quincy who was sleeping peaceful next to me.

"Babe, my kids will be up in a second, you have to get ready to leave okay?"

He looked up at me and told me that he was going to take a shower and put on some clothes but he was not going anywhere. I was puzzled and not in the mood to fight his ass so I let him talk. "Listen Momma, I think that fucking baby is mine and I'm definitely going to be an active father. I don't care what you got going on or who you fucking at the moment. I know you want to protect the other kids but I'm coming around and when I do for mine, I'm gonna help you with them too. That's just the kind of man I am. So my nigga, you can get your fat Booty ass in this shower with me, put on some clothes, get ready to introduce me to those lil ones and we finna plan us a lil family day. K, cool! Oh! And those fucking other niggas are done; I ain't having that shit." He let a loud, YES SIR and hopped out the bed.

We got in the shower and I proceeded to ask him what he was going to do about his fiancé. He let me know that he was going to have a tough conversation with her. He said that he loved her but he could never be in love with her because I had his heart. Quincy turned to face me and said, "From the first time you walked your lil short ass down to my department and started telling us to watch our back because those white boys stayed in the office telling on us, I knew I wanted you. You too cool and you are always looking out for the under dogs. I tried to fight the urge and shit, you know, be respectful of your marriage but when we ended up fucking, I fell in love with you. You know I come from a two parent home and I was not raised to break up families so that's why I had to pull away. I met shawty, we kicked it and fucked around until we got serious. But to be honest, I keep looking for you in her and that's not fair to her. I gotta let her go because I can't let yo ass go. I don't care if that baby ain't mine, we gone figure this shit out together. I know I gotta be reasonable and give you some time to sort this shit out so Ima do that but I'm letting you know in the end it's gonna be me and you!"

He gave me a long french kiss, splashed water in my eyes on purpose, then started washing his balls. I thought to myself, damn I love this man.

I put on my clothes and walked with Quincy to the living room in just enough time. The kids flew out of their room running toward me while looking at him.

"Come on in here babies, this is Mama's friend Quincy."

My son Darion just stared, he was my little protector and he wanted to know who this strange man was standing in their hotel room while they were on vacation. My baby girl Maddie looked and said hey and grabbed me by the waist. She was a daddy's girl so she wasn't too fond of another man being around her Mama. My oldest, Amari, looked at me then looked at him and said, "well he's cute or whatever" she then started laughing. She was my silly one who was at the age where she loved to look at the fellas and gawk.

We all laughed and the day was a ball from there. We ordered breakfast from room service and I explained that Quincy was my friend who I used to work with and he was in town for vacation like us. I let them know that he didn't have anyone come with him so I invited him to have a little fun with us. They were cool with it and started naming things that we could do for that day. After we ate it was time to hit those California streets and enjoy some sunny D.

Chapter 29

Quincy became our own personal tour guide aka bodyguard for the rest of our trip. It felt like we were one happy family. Even when the kids and I would go on vacation with my husband, I never felt like him and I were a complete family. He was boring, he never had an idea of what we should do while there and we never had any type of sexual interaction while on vacation. With Quincy, as the days went by, we became lovey dovey and couldn't keep our hands off each other. We spent our day time doing so many fun things and whatever the kids wanted to do to wear them out by the time we made it back to the suite; our nights always belonged to us. Although he had a room at the other hotel, he never went back to sleep there after our first night together. We fucked the shit out of each other every night for the duration of the trip. I fell more and more in love with that man and the thought of us parting ways made me emotional. I couldn't see myself being with anyone else but him so I knew I had to figure out how in the hell I was going to tell both Kelton and Davion that this baby I was carrying isn't theirs and to never contact me again without having to run for my life. I didn't want to get Quincy involved because I knew if anything went down he wouldn't hesitate to show his natural black ass about me. I didn't want to put him in danger.

I laid in the bed after a streaming round of bathroom sex looking at the ceiling. Quincy could see that my mind was racing and asked what was going on in my head.

"I'm just laying here wondering how I'm gonna clean up this mess I've made with my life Papi. I mean, I have to tell lying ass Davion which I'm not worried about. I'm worried about Kelton, he is a ticking time bomb and so unpredictable. I could be getting away with pulling the gun out on his Pops Jerome but I'd definitely have to use that bitch fucking with that bipolar ass Gemini Kelton."

I started crying, Quincy pulled me into his arms and whispered in me ear, "I understand that you have a lot of shit going on but hear me clearly, I will fuck every last one of them up if they try to do anything to you and that's on my Mama and unborn child. Every last one of them niggas will be in a fucking casket dawg."

He wiped my face with his hands and told me to chill out and enjoy the rest of my night.

His comfort turned me on so bad, I gave him the best sloppy top he had ever had in his life and went to sleep.

We got up the next morning and we briefly discussed what we planned on doing to end our situations back home and that he would be coming to the house to spend time with the kids and I weekly. I was so giddy like a schoolgirl. I was finally getting the man I had desired for years and I couldn't wait to be his Mrs.

Chapter 30

We said our "see you laters" at the airport, the kiddos and I headed home. Our first stop was to my Granny's house to check in with her. I knew my mother was gonna be there because I spoke to her while we were at LAX. She informed me that she was in town for a couple of weeks to see her mama, her kids, and her grand babies. It had been almost 5 months since I had seen my mom because like me, she was a very successful entrepreneur. She stayed on the go creating generational wealth for us. Even if I had decided I wanted to be a bomb, I would have never had to worry about money or taking care of my babies. My Mama would always hold me down whether my Dad stepped up or not. I had gotten to the point where I just wanted to be around the people that made me feel safe.

My Granny and my Mom would sacrifice their life for me so it was always a pleasure to see them. We also were able to eat some of that delicious food my Mom had prepared for us. She was the successful local business owner of one of the most famous restaurant chains in the south called Maddie's

Soul Food. People would travel miles just to get a taste of her fried chicken, ribs, Boston butt sandwiches, mac & cheese, sweet potato soufflé, and famous Maddie's Spicy Sauce. I could cook but I didn't have anything on my Mama's food. My kids ate like I had starved them the entire 3 weeks we were gone. We took our time and enjoyed each other's company after my belly got full and I decided we were gonna go ahead and spend a night. That night turned into staying there until my Mama got ready to leave which ended up being another 3 weeks. You can do what you want when you're the boss and that's just what I had started doing. I called all of the stores and had a conference call with everyone on my management team. I informed them that my doctor classified me as a high risk pregnancy and put me on bedrest. Another lie being told. I told them that I didn't know when I would be allowed to come back to work but I knew that they would have the company operating as if I was there. I let Sarah know that she needed to step up and make sure the tasks I normally completed were done by her. She knew exactly what to do and how to do everything plus I could trust her. I told her after the conference call that I needed her to call me personally to follow up.

Everyone wished me well and the call ended, Sarah called me shortly afterwards and I started asking her questions! I didn't want her to know anything other than what I had told everyone else but I needed to know what I would be walking into when I did decide to come back.

"Sarah, thank you for stepping up to the plate for me. I know that you can handle it but one quick question; do Jerome and Kelton still show up to work?"

"Wait a minute! What the hell done happened Tine?"

Damn! I told you, it was always hard getting something past her ass but I was going to stick to my guns and try to convince her ass that it was nothing!

"Damn Gul! Nothing? You know I've been gone a long time; I really haven't been bothered so I haven't answered their calls."

She quickly let out a sound that let me know she felt like I was full of shit. She then told me that both of them had been reporting to work on time and that they had been getting on her damn nerves questioning her about me.

My heart dropped, I was hoping Jerome would have taken his ass somewhere. I told her that I appreciated her more than she would ever know and I would let her come to see me when I was in a better mood. I knew that I didn't have too long to go without seeing her before she started spazing. Our phone call was interrupted by a customer needing her so she had to get off the phone. I went back to enjoying my family that day and didn't answer the phone for no one but Quincy, Sarah, Tiffani and my other friends the duration of my time away.

I was at peace and it turned out to be my calm before the storm.

Chapter 31

After my Mom left, me and the kids went back home and packed up our personal things. I had decided that it was time to move. I didn't feel safe in my home anymore because Jerome knew where I lived and considering how close Kelton was from me, he had to know as well. If he didn't, I'm sure his Pops wouldn't mind telling him. I also didn't want to start my life over and have Quincy living in that house with my kids and I. Every chance he got, Davion would have something to say about that. Well, that's whenever he finally decided to come around. I had found a new home about forty-five minutes away that was closer toward Quincy's hometown and were able to move in within two days, thanks to him and his homeboys. Since we had gotten back from Cali, as the days passed, I had fallen more and more in love with that man. He made me feel like a schoolgirl head over hills with a star player on the football team. He was the grand prize and all he wanted was me. We had an emotional connection, our alignment and intimacy went beyond just physical attraction, we were having fun together, surface-level conversations and intellectual similarities. We connected on a deeper level. He was my soulmate and I was his.

I had a conversation with him about his status with his ex-fiancé and he told me that she was still out on a mission trip in Africa but she was due back in the next couple of days. He assured me that he was going to have the tough conversation with her as soon as she got back in town. He said in the meantime he was going to move in with me because I deserved to have someone holding me and making my kids and I feel safe every night. Time was flying by and another two weeks had gone by.

That Sunday I had finally received a phone call from Davion asking where the kids and I were. I had every intention of contacting him but I had no thought of him with Quincy around. He explained to me that he had tried to stop by the house but was informed by Roger, the gate security officer that we no longer lived there. The good thing about having the home in only my name meant that I didn't have to discuss renting or selling the house with him. I had the right to do what the fuck I wanted with it. That is until we proceeded with the divorce, which I intended on doing that week. I could tell by the sound of his voice that he was defeated and felt extremely guilty so I felt I had a better chance at getting whatever I wanted. I also wanted to make the process quick. I told him that I was selling the home and that we needed to get as far away from that place as quickly as possible. The truth is, I had no plans to sell my house, I just wanted him to never be able to connect me to it again.

He sounded like all the air was let out of him. He began to apologize for not being able to live up to the expectations of the man I deserved. He told me that Chantelle was just a slut who threw herself at him one day and had gotten pregnant. He said that at that moment, he was weak and that he didn't know what to do because he didn't want to break my heart and end our marriage. Before he could get anything else out I quickly cut him off and let him know that the only thing we needed to discuss from that point was our divorce and our kids. I didn't want to talk about my cousin Chantelle because the whole family knew she was the family's whore. She'd sleep with a dog if money was involved. I was definitely going to check her and let my Mom and Granny know what the tramp had been up to. He could forget it, there was no way in hell I was going to let his ass see me sweat about her. Fuck her! He'd have to wait until the divorce proceedings to hear me read his ass about her.

We agreed to meet up at my Granny's home so he could see the kids and take them if they wanted to go the next day. I wasn't prepared for his appearance.

Chapter 32

It was evident that Davon was going through pure hell. He looked like he had aged ten years since I'd last saw him. He had bags under his eyes as if he hadn't slept in weeks, he had dropped about twenty pounds and his clothes were barely staying on his frail body. His appearance made my heart drop. I actually became overwhelmed with the sadness he exuded. My husband had always been a kept man. From head to toe everyday he dressed in the latest fashions and every time he walked in the room, heads would turn because he smelled so damn good. Now, he was broken-hearted and you could physically see his distress. He had lost the one thing that used to mean the most to him and he believed it was all his fault. I knew in his mind, he had become the failure his father was and that was the last person he always told me he wanted to emulate.

Part of me wanted to hug him and reassure him that everything was going to be okay. No matter how hurt and mad I was, seeing anyone so broken could never bring me pleasure, especially the father of my kids.

While Maddie and Darion acted as if everything was normal, Amari who is a carbon-copy of me, immediately noticed the difference in her Dad's appearance and became vocal about it.

"Daddy, what is wrong with you? Where have you been and why do you look so sick?"

Davon knew his daughter better than anyone and he was going to address her without holding back. His answer let me know that he was fully prepared for her.

"Baby girl, Daddy did some things that he is not too proud of and now I have to deal with the consequences of my actions. I am simply having a hard time with not being able to be around you all."

She looked over at him and replied, "Well what did you do to us that was so horrible Daddy, whatever you did had to be bad because Mama done went and got herself a new man"

I quickly cut her little ass off and told him that I had ran into Quinton while we were on vacation and he took us around to sight see the area. Quinton was my gay friend who lived in Cali. My ass had become so fluent at telling lies it was a shame. I looked at Amari and gave her that look that let her know to shut the hell up. She knew not to tell her Dad any more of my business or she was going to get her ass beat. She talked too much; she was not about to blow up my spot before I could complete what I had strategically planned out.

116

Davion asked me if it would be okay to take the kids shopping and out to the movies. I agree because I wanted to enjoy some alone time with Quincy after he got off of work. After they left I received a phone call from Kelton telling me that we needed to talk. I thought to myself, "I do not have time for his shit today" so I told him that I would meet him at a park right around from his apartment. When I got there the first thing he did was pull me in to kiss me. I tried to pull away but he overpowered me. He slid his tongue down my throat and I had no choice but to go with the flow. I didn't want Kelton to touch me at all, let alone kiss me but I didn't want to cause a scene.

"Where the fuck have you been and why you ain't told me what's been going on with you and my child?" Kelton said as he caressed my belly when he finally came up for air.

The way he looked into my eyes like he was torn between being both frustrated and concerned was sexy as fuck, I can't lie. I told him that things had gotten very crazy at home mixed with my pregnancy being very difficult because of my age. I told him that I needed time to be alone because I was just going through too much and I didn't want to continue to have a relationship with him. A part of me wanted to let him know that I had planned to be with the love of my life and whether the baby was his or not, my lover was going to raise the child but I knew he'd try to break my

117

neck so I shut the hell up after that. Kelton looked at me and told me that I was just talking nonsense because my hormones were all over the place. He then demanded that I get into his car. I was confused and scared at the same time but I complied. When we arrived at the destination, I realized he had taken me to Cheaha State Park. This negro had taken me 2,407 above sea level and my dumb ass let him. It was getting dark and I was so scared I could have pissed my pants. He ordered me out of the car and into a room he had reserved beforehand. When I stepped into the door Kelton had the place decked out with rose petals everywhere, lit candles and a chef who had prepared a beautiful spread of food. I sat in the chair and ate my food as Luther Vandross played in the background. After we ate our dinner when the chef stepped out of the room, Kelton grabbed my hand and pulled me into him. He gently started kissing me from my lips to my belly, then he pulled my pencil skirt up, slid my panties to the side, and kissed my pussy lips. My body quivered and I became weak at the knees.

Chapter 33

When his long penis penetrated me, a loud moan came out of my mouth. I could not believe my dumb ass was up in this room allowing that man to fuck me yet again. I immediately felt regretful. I pushed him off of me and told him to take me home. Kelton acted as if he was beyond confused and I didn't care. I no longer felt the need to explain anything to him. I repeated myself and the second time, my voice was more stern.

He grabbed his hair and said "Oh my fucking God, what is your problem now, please don't stop me right now." He looked like a kid that was on the verge of having a temper tantrum because his favorite toy was getting taken away. He was use to me letting him have his way, he thought that I was going to give in. I wasn't and I didn't.

He looked at me than grabbed me by the neck and slammed me against the wall. While having his face inches away from mine he stated, "Man you so damn stupid, with your slutty ass. I will fuck you up in this room. I know yo ass running around fucking other niggas with my baby in you, you dirty whore."

I could feel his spit and hot breath hit my face with each word, I was terrified of him. He was strong and there was no way I could defend myself against him so I just let him say and do what he wanted. He forced his penis in me and started pounding my vagina. He pumped and pumped until he nutted inside of me. With his hand still wrapped around my neck, he told me that my sweet pussy would always be his and that he would blow my brains out if he ever found out that I was giving it to anyone else. After what felt like five long ass minutes, I felt myself losing consciences. I guess he felt my body becoming limp because he released me by throwing me across the room and onto the bed. Although the bed was soft, the land was hard and on my stomach I went. Pain shot up my stomach and down my back. I let out the loudest scream I could muster up because he was crazy and I knew that my life depended on it. Thank God a house keeper was walking by at that exact moment and heard me. Unbeknownst to me at the time, she had immediately ran to the front desk and called local police to come and intervene. As I laid there getting cursed out some more while in pain with blood running down my thighs, several police officers came up to the door and knocked.

One of them yelled out, "We got a call about a disturbance, we need someone to open the door so that we can make sure everything is ok".

My heart dropped because I did not want them to come into the room and take his life. Even though I wasn't sure if my baby was still alive or not, I was worried about him and his black ass. He walked over to a chair he had thrown across the room, he put his shirt on and started to put his pants on as he yelled for the officers to give him one second. If looks could kill, I'd be dead as a door knob because he gave me the nastiest look I had ever been given. He turned his nose up at me and whispered, "If you say anything to them I'm gonna fuck yo ass up you dumb bitch."

I was extremely scared and I was crying, as soon as he opened the door I leaped out of the bed with the sheet wrapped around me. I was so glad to see several black officers standing there because if they were white, I probably would have been shot down like a dog in the street. I screamed, "Please help me, he's assaulting me and I'm scared for my life."

Kelton sat on the edge of the bed and bit his bottom lip as if he were in disbelief. As two of the officers walked over toward him and told him to stand up and put his hands behind his back, the other two grabbed me and asked me to lay on the bed until the EMT arrived. I knew that I was bleeding but I didn't realize just how much until I followed the two officer's eyes that were looking down at my legs. I started freaking out, I didn't care if the baby was Kelton's or not, it was my baby and I didn't want anything to happen to my baby. As Kelton was being led to the cop's car, I called Quincy. He picked up on the first ring. I yelled into the phone for him to come to the hotel on the mountain. I couldn't control myself so the officer took the phone and gave him all the information he needed, after he asked Quincy who he was to me. The EMT arrived minutes later and to my surprise, so did Quincy. He was a nervous wreck and I felt like shit for putting him through this. I was put on a stretcher and taken to the local hospital. Quincy was with me the entire time and I was beyond thankful for him and his presence.

Chapter 34

I was in so much pain that I passed out while in the ambulance. By the time I woke up, we had made it to the hospital and the doctors had ran every test needed to ensure my baby was perfectly fine. They had inserted me with an IV and had given me some mild pain meds to help with the soreness. I looked over at Quincy and whisper, I have to call my babies. He leaned over and kissed me on the forehead and stated, "it's already taken care of, your husband is aware that you are in the hospital. I let him know that you were attacked by an obsessed co-worker while exercising in the park. I told him that I was a friend of yours from work and the police called me because I was the last person that you had received a call from. We were talking about property if he need to give out any more details to make your story believable. He is on his way to see you so relax and just go with my story baby." He then leaned over and kissed my lips and told me to get some rest until he got there. That man had sat up there and came up with a whole lie to cover my ass when he knew what the real deal was. Every time I was around him and he would breath I fell more and more in love with his ass.

Davion came into the room about an hour after I had dozed back off, Quincy was still sitting by my side and from the look on his face, he had no plans of leaving. Davion walked up to him, gave him a hand shake and thank him for being by my side. He looked at me and tried to rub my face, but I quickly snatched away. I looked at Davion and told him to not touch me. He knew I did not like that shit and the fact that he had probably had his fingers all in my cousin's pussy, that was a hell no! I then asked him where my babies were. He let me know that he had taken them to my Granny's house and that she had called my mother and sister who were on their way. He said that she was so worried that she had even called my Daddy who let it be known; he most definitely would be coming into town as soon as possible. Because they all didn't live in the same state I knew that I didn't have to worry about answering questions until tomorrow at least. It was about to be a shit show when my Mama and Daddy ended up in the same room tho. Although they were both Cancers and their birthdays were days apart, they were totally opposite of each other and couldn't get along for shit. They had been separated since I was a baby and always got along up until my Daddy decided to marry Lisa whore ass. On a family trip to go see him, I had decided that it would be a great idea to invite my friend who was more like a cousin to me to my Dad's house because it had been a year since I had last seen her. She was my sister's real cousin on her Dad's side of the family. My mother had taken her in to help her get out of an abusive relationship and get back on her feet. While living with my Mama, she decided that she was in love with my Granny's brother. That shit lasted for only one year and he sent her back down south to her parents' house. He had caught her cheating, lying and stealing money from him. I didn't know all of that at the time and thought that my family was just taking my Uncle's side because he was family. She was my friend, I loved her, and I was going to have her back so I did and that was a big mistake. When she walked into my Daddy's house he started acting giddy like a school boy that was willing to do anything and fuck everyone over to have a piece of her. I vividly remember Davion leaning over and telling me, "You know your Daddy and Lisa are going to hook up, don't you?" Me being naive as hell, I looked at him and told him that she would never do that to me but in reality, that bitch didn't give a fuck about me, my Mama, or her own flesh and blood, my sister. Within two days after I had left, I got on Facebook and saw pictures of them on date after date. He was proud of his whore and he wanted the world to see her. My Mama was so hurt because this was a person that she had known, she had a child with Lisa's

125

cousin, she took her and her kids in and she was married into our family.

One day shit hit the fan, they were cursing each other out on Facebook and I was horrified. I couldn't believe some of the things my Daddy was saying to my Mama and about her. He accused her of being jealous and he allowed Lisa to disrespect her as well. My Mama was trying to warn him that Lisa was no good, did not like working, was known for laying on her back to get a dollar and her and her kids would have him tied up in all kinds of legal shit. One thing is for sure, my mother was no saint and she had done things that she wasn't too proud of but she was never jealous of Lisa, Lisa never had shit a hard working woman like my Mama would want and if she did she could go get it herself. That included my Daddy's whore-ish ass. My Mama is a real woman that is about her business. My Mama wasn't a low life sneaky whore who would fuck over any and every-one to get her way and be with a man that wasn't going to do anything but end up beating her ass when he found out her true character and got tired of her crap. My Daddy and Lisa were both delusional and full of shit.

After calling me one day to explain to me that they only were concerned about me and my feelings, I had made the decision that I was never allowing them around me again. My exact thoughts were, if you don't give a damn about my sister, your own flesh and blood who I'd kill for. If you don't give a damn about my Mama, the only mother I will ever have and one of the two only people that have consistently had my back, the woman who took her dusty ass in. You damn sure don't give a damn about me. They could both kiss my ass a thousand times and go straight to hell for all I care.

Chapter 35

S o there I laid in the hospital bed with Quincy's sexy ass sitting to my right and Davion's dusty ass sitting to the left. After about two hours of them sitting there having a conversation that was only interesting to them, as if I didn't exist. Davion finally looked at me and said that he was going to go ahead and go get the kids. He let me know that he would bring them back up there tomorrow after school. Quincy intercepted the conversation and said that he was about to head out as well because his fiancé had just gotten into town and he was about to go meet her. He told me that he would call me to check on me from time to time. My fucking heart dropped. The audacity of his ass, I thought. All I know was, he better be on his way to let that trick know that their engagement was over with and nothing more. When he and Davion left out of my room, I laid in bed and thought of all the crazy crap I had gotten myself into. All I could do was lay there and cry. Just when I started feeling sorry for myself because my life was a complete mess, I heard a knock on the door. I attempted to sit up but instantly felt sharp pains travel up my spine so I slid back down and yelled, "Come in."

To my surprise, in walked Jerome! I immediately reached for the phone to call the front desk so someone could help me get his ass out of my room. I guess he read my mind because he quickly and in a soft spoken voice said, "Don't call them, I'm not here to hurt you baby, I would never hurt you Tina, why do I have to keep telling you that."

My eyes rolled hard as hell when he stated that. This nigga must had forgotten that he had not too long ago pulled a gun out on me. The fact that I was in a hospital bed because of his son was enough for me. He had to be crazy to think I wasn't thinking he was there to finish me off. All the energy I had completely left my body so I laid there and just stared at him as he talked. "This shit is crazy and it is beyond out of hand. Someone is going to get killed if all of us don't stop Tina. The police had Kelton in custody with a twenty-thousand-dollar bond that I plan on posting tonight. I've always been transparent with you and I'm not going to stop now. All of this is not your fault, I know this because we have all played a part in it. We have got to stop this shit! I will take care of my child and he will never put his fucking hands on you again, that's a promise. I gonna need for you to stop fucking my son. After you have this baby, we are going to get a DNA test. If it's his, we will make sure it's taking care of. If

129

it's not, we will make sure we leave you the fuck alone. All I'm asking is that you do your part in making sure you don't contact him. I never thought in a million years that we would end up like this but here we are. I love you and you will always be a great friend of mine, even if you got all of us running around chasing yo ass like we are bat shit crazy. This just has to stop, you were only supposed to give him some pussy and let his ass go on about his business. What the fuck were you doing to my child in that bedroom to make him lose his fucking mind like that? Why did we have to get here? Well never mind, shit almost drove me crazy." Jerome looked up at me with sexy eyes and started chuckling and finished what he was saying. "I don't want to see anything happen to you baby, so please help me stop this shit."

My body was extremely tense because of his presence and he noticed. He walked over to the chair that was placed by my hospital bed and slid it closer to me, then he sat in it. Just as he was getting ready to say something else to me. Quincy walked back into the room. He looked over at Jerome then back at me, "Tina, who is this?" Without hesitation, I let him know that it was Kelton's dad, Jerome. Quincy looked back up at Jerome and told him that he needed to slide back from my bed. As he was talking, he started walking toward Jerome. The thought of them tearing my hospital room up and causing a scene gave me all the energy I needed to sit my ass up in that bed and yell at them not to start acting a fool. They scared me to the point that I started crying, my voice and body was trembling.

Jerome looked from Quincy to me, in a calm tone he let us both know that he did not come up there to hurt me or start any type of shit. I assume by the way he was looking at me, he had put two and two together and realized who Quincy was so he understood why he was acting so protective over me. He grabbed my hand and asked, "Does he know?" As I was pulling my hand away from his, I replied, "Yes, he knows everything. He is the love of my life and no matter who this baby belongs to, Quincy and I will raise it. Speaking of my baby, it is doing just fine considering the fact that your son tried to make me lose it. Now, I will not be fucking your crazy abusive son anymore so you don't ever have to worry about that. Hell, I will never fuck you again. Once I have this baby, I will contact you so the DNA test can be completed. Other than that, I ask that you do not attempt to contact me again." I laid my ass back in the bed and watched Quincy roll his eyes at Jerome as he got up and started leaving out of the room without uttering another word. As soon as the door shut, he looked over at me and said, "You and that pussy been very busy fucking niggas up in the head. It's time for you to sit yo ass down because I'm not gonna deal with you fucking these niggas and coming back to me."

I looked at him and in full agreement I said, "Yes sir."

I immediately laid back and fell asleep.

Chapter 36

By the time I woke back up it was the next day and Quincy was laying on my bed holding me tightly. I looked at his face as he slept and thought about how blessed I was to have a man like him supporting me and loving me through this situation. He was the most thoughtful human I had ever met and the fact that he would still choose me when he knew the full details of my prior scandalized endeavors was mind-blowing. He loved me without judgement and I would love him for eternity because of it.

My Mama burst through the door with my sister and kids in tow.

"Tina! Who in the hell is this and what is going on baby? Her loud voice made Quincy leap out of his sleep. For some reason, I was tickled by his reaction. I started laughing uncontrollably as my kids leaped over to hug him. They were so happy to see him and they didn't even acknowledge the fact that I was laid up in the hospital bed.

"Mama, this is my friend Quincy, he has been here making sure I'm safe. And you are so loud, stop acting like that." I was interrupted my sister Quanesha, " Ummm girl, fuck all that, hell you know she loud and she worried about you. I wanna get to the point and find out who I done came up here to fuck up because somebody getting their ass shot today." My hazel eyed sister was just as beautiful as she wanted to be. Hair hung past her butt and her skin was a light toned caramel color. We both were blessed with nice plump pear shaped bottoms I had more ass but her stomach was as flat as an ironing board because she didn't have any kids. She could have been a model or a sugar baby because of her looks but she was one of the "hoodest" people you could meet. Sweet and rough around the edges. We had made it out of the ghetto many years ago but for some reason you would think she was still living in the Cooper Homes projects with the way she would cut up when someone pissed her off. She would run a wealthy man off with the quickness because they had too much to lose. She often rotated a hood boy who did whatever the hell she told him to do. Quincy had never met my family before and this was definitely not the way I wanted him to. I knew if I started naming people my sister would call her goon friends and all hell would break loose so I decided that was going to give them the watered down version of what the hell I had been up to. I started with my trifling cousin Chantelle who I hadn't had a chance to confront about her shady ass fucking my husband. I knew my sister's

134

first stop would be to her house to give her an old fashion ass whooping and that's exactly where I wanted her to start.

Just as I was wrapping up the story, my Daddy and his whore walked in. He was so focused on me and didn't see my Mom and my sister standing by the door. Before he could utter a word to me, my Mama and my sister leaped at them and all hell broke out. My sister grabbed her cousin, my Mama grabbed my Daddy and I motioned for my kids to stand closer to me. During their Facebook showdown, my Mama told him she was gonna beat him and his slut up on sight and that's exactly what she meant. I could not get up and risk hurting myself and more importantly, my unborn child. Quincy sprang into action to make sure my Daddy didn't hit my Mama who was tearing his ass up. The first kick to his balls took him down and it was a lost cause from then on. She used every move she had on him and even if he wanted to, he couldn't handle her. I didn't know she was so good at throwing them hands the way she did. My eyes went from them to my sister. She was sitting on top of Lisa pounding her head when the hospital police officers barged into the room and helped Quincy separate everyone. Lisa had all that mouth but let my sister who was half her age beat the hell out of her. My Daddy was so pissed off, he told his wife to pick her purse up so they could get the fuck out of there. Years would go by before I saw or spoke to him again.

Chapter 37

I stayed in the hospital for a week before I was released but I was bed ridden for two weeks and then put on light duty for the duration of my pregnancy. Due to all of the circumstances, I was considered extremely high risk and my doctor didn't want to chance me losing the baby. I was able to settle the divorce from Davion within one month after my release because he didn't contest it. His guilt made him agree to give me everything I had asked for, including full custody of the kids. I was not a bitch, so he knew he would not have any trouble seeing the kids when he wanted to. I had only requested ten thousand in alimony and ten for child support, which was pennies to him. I'm sure that helped him agree to my terms.

During that time, Quincy also called off the engagement with his fiancé Angelica.

From his side of the story, she took it hard but understood that he was not in love with her and didn't want to waste her time. He told her he didn't want to keep her from her true soulmate, true love and happiness. He told her

136

he couldn't live without me and that we had a baby on the way. I didn't give a damn what he had to tell her, I just want their relationship over with and I wanted my man all to myself. I'm a woman first so I felt bad for her, but I loved that man way more than she ever could and I was with him before she was thought about. He was mine and had always been.

Quincy had packed up all of his belongings, rented out his home and moved in with me. I had set up visitation arrangements with Jerome and we agreed that he would pick the kids up every other weekend. So, when he showed up at my door on a Wednesday morning, I was puzzled. Before I had the chance to answer the door, Quincy did.

"What's up man, what brought you here today?"

As I eased around the corner, I heard Davion reply, "So how long you've been fucking my wife nigga and don't lie because I heard it was way before we even thought about getting a divorce!"

Holding my stomach, I walked up and stood next to Quincy. Why me Lord! I thought to myself. I didn't even get a chance to open my mouth, Davion looked at me and asked me, "So Tina, who's fucking baby is it? Is it mine, is it his, is it Jerome, or is it Kelton? Tell the truth bitch before I kill you today."

Who the fuck has he been talking to, I thought to myself while looking at him. Next thing I remember was Quincy yelling, in a deep voice, "Bitch you ain't gone touch her and don't you ever come up in our house disrespecting my woman." In mid-sentence, he swung at Davion and knocked him to the floor. There was no way I was gonna stand there and let them fight like two niggas in the street with my kids up stairs. I ran to the kitchen and pulled my gun out of my purse and pointed it at Davion, "Y'all please stop, please. We can talk about this like three adults. Please stop before my babies hear us and come down here." Quincy was beating his ass and that shit made my pussy start throbbing but I had to refocus and stop this shit show before someone ended up dead for real. I kept the gun aimed at Davion and I told him that if he couldn't come at me correct that I would be issuing a restraining order on his ass by tomorrow. He got his beat-up self off the floor and stood next to the door. "Tina, what the fuck have you been up to? From what I've found out, you've been fucking niggas all over town. Shid! Did you know that playa?" I looked at Quincy and answered for him, "Yes, I've been in a couple of entanglements and this man, my true love, knows all about every last one of them. So you want to know whose baby this is, well here is some honesty for your ass. It could be Kelton's or it could by

138

Quincy's. One thing for sure; it ain't yours and I'm thankful to God for that.

Davion dropped his head and started crying. I was so pissed at the way he came into my house so I wanted to light his ass up with the gun I was still holding in my hand. "Do you have anything else you need to know before I call the police on you Davion, because you have some nerve coming over here acting a fool like you ain't been fucking my stank ass cousin." Rolling my eyes as the words left my mouth.

Davion looked from me to Quincy and Quincy back to me. "I could fuck a million women and none of them would compare to you Tina. You have been and you will always be the reason I live. I will never give up on us and I don't care who you are with or who you marry, you will always be the love of my life and my wife." He turned around and walked out of the door looking to defeated.

Chapter 38

Quincy closed his eyes and said to himself, "What the fuck have I gotten myself into."

My heart felt like it was breaking into pieces because I never wanted him to regret being with me. I never wanted him to second guess his decision to walk away from someone that could have been a better partner than I. He was such an awesome, understanding and stable man. He deserved nothing but a high quality woman standing by his side as his mate. I grabbed him by the hand and led him to our bedroom. I told him that I would be right back and went to see what the kids were up to. Thankfully, they were sound asleep. I put my gun back into my purse and went back into my room where he was sitting on the bedside. While softly kissing on his ear I whispered, "everything you need me to be, I will be that. I promise to honor you, respect you, and submit to you. The love we have for each other is unmatched, I thank you for showing me the definition of unconditional. Now I'm ready to fuck my man's brains out." Quincy started smiling and got butt booty naked. I dropped down on my knees and started tonguing his penis like I was a pornstar. With every kiss, suck and lick he would moan. I wanted to make love to him with my mouth. I wanted him to feel my love through every stroke. I wanted to apologize and let the oral sex do the talking. "Fuck baby, you be sucking the shit out of me, damn you gone make me cum quick as fuck if you keep doing this shit." I started moaning and licking his balls and moaning and sucking his dick even more. I looked up at him and said," I know this shit feel too good Papi, I wanna feel this big black dick bust all in my mouth, do it for Momma." That line took him out and his orgasm was one for the books. As I was getting up, Quincy scooped me up and put me in the bed. He got next to me and stared at me for what seemed like 10 minutes. Just as I had started feeling uncomfortable he began asking me how did I plan on telling all these motherfukers what was really up. He let me know that shit could not continue to go like it was going and I 100 percent agreed with him. The last thing I wanted was for anyone of them to end up hurt or dead because of my actions. People act out of emotions so I wasn't going to stay mad at either of them. Even Kelton, even though he tried to kill me. I don't know why but something about that man made me love his ass as unconditionally as Quincy, Davion, and Jerome loved me. I wanted to end the confusion so I decided I was going to talk to my doctor about getting a

141

DNA test while I was still pregnant. I let him know that I was going to schedule an appointment and I would let him know the date so that he could accompany me. He gently kissed my lips and continued to stare at me. That time I felt at ease, even though he didn't utter another word, I knew that he was just admiring me from the glaze that sat in his eyes. In that moment, I felt safe, I felt peace.

Acknowledgements

Tina's Escapades was co-inspired by my sister, Quanesha Dimming-Curry. Without you the title and leading lady, Tina, would not exist. Thank you my forever baby girl.

Thank you to my husband Ricko for your unwavering support with all of my endeavors. I couldn't have asked for a more patient and supportive partner than you. I love you.

To my kids Amari, Darion, and Zyria, you three became my reason when I birth you. Your mother is beyond grateful for you and don't you ever forget that. Our deep conversations, the way you guys jump into any situation to help me out, and our time spent running through the house like kids on a playground make my heart smile. You all make me smile from the inside out. God sent me his angels when he gave me you.

To my Mother Aretha, my Granny Stella, and my Daddy Anthony, the phone calls, social media re-shares, and excitement when you call me about my projects are overwhelming in the best way. My goal is to make you proud to have me as your daughter and your gleeful conversations let me know that I am on the right track.

Everyone needs a Tiffani ! Having someone that genuinely has your back in every situation is a blessing. You are a treasure in my life, and I am grateful for all that you do.

To Antonio Stew, Donna, Audry, Shakearra, Malcolm, Sarah, Chrissy, TK, Toinetta, Ann, Ashley, Cam, Eric, Munster, Niya, Maya, Eriica, my goal sisters, and a host of other supportive friends. There are days that the sun refuse to shine but your love, support, and encouraging words always seem to brighten my day. I pray I am as much of a blessing to each of you as you are to me.

Safira Okkyone
THE AUTHOR

www.ingramcontent.com/pod-product-compliance
Lightning Source LLC
Chambersburg PA
CBHW060424260626
47161CB00005B/1766